MW01621179

A SMALL LIGHT IN THE DARKNESS

A SMALL LIGHT IN THE DARKNESS

AND OTHER SHORT STORIES BY JACK WEYLAND

Deseret Book Company
Salt Lake City, Utah

The following stories are used by permission of The Church of Jesus Christ of Latter-day Saints:

"A Small Light in the Darkness"
"Saturday Morning Fever"
"Sometimes They Call Me Brother"
"The Quiet War"
"Companions"
"Jeremy Cargo—Live for the First Time in Utah"
"The Gimmick"
"Happiest Two Years"
"The Goldfish Parable"
"Afterwards Refreshments Will Be Served"
"Letters from a Loving Brother"
"Lookin' Good"
"And When the Night Came"
"A Chance to Make Good"

First printing October 1987
Second printing January 1988

Library of Congress Cataloging-in-Publication Data

Weyland, Jack, 1940–
A small light in the darkness.

Summary: A collection of sixteen short stories portraying Mormon youth in contemporary situations that test and prove their faith.

1. Mormons—Juvenile fiction. 2. Christian fiction. [1. Mormons—Fiction. 2. Christian life—Fiction. 3. Short stories] I. Title.
PZ7.W538Sm 1987 [Fic] 87-22281
ISBN 0-87579-105-0

Contents

A Small Light in the Darkness

The first night in their new home the family slept on the floor in sleeping bags because the moving van hadn't arrived with the furniture. The next morning, during the brief interval between sleep and consciousness when he first opened his eyes, Kyle couldn't remember where he was. From his viewpoint on the floor of the empty bedroom, the walls seemed to converge at strange, distorted angles high above him. A single shaft of sunlight swept bright and dark patterns across the floor and wall. Small dust particles exposed by the light danced—as if to the music of a silent song.

Then, as a dream only vaguely recalled, the memory of leaving their home seeped into his mind—the awkward last few words with his friends in the priests quorum, each aware of a deep bond built over years of camping, sports, and priesthood activities. Embarrassed to put words to what they felt, they finally resorted to lame jokes and a last, clumsy, hurried handshake. Then the drive by car. His father had let Kyle drive partway down the four-lane ribbon that crossed the rolling plains leading east to Illinois.

Kyle brought the cover of the sleeping bag to his face, taking in the delicious smell of campfires in the mountains fifty miles from his old home. He wondered if his friend Jed back home had gone camping last night.

First published in the *New Era*, September 1985

Kyle remembered the first time he had seen Jed. It was when they were both nine years old. A boy from a new family in the neighborhood had walked across the street and watched Kyle practice doing chin-ups on the branch of a tree in the front yard.

"How many can you do?" Jed had asked.

"Twenty," Kyle had answered.

"That's not so many. I can do thirty."

By the day's end, they were both doing forty chin-ups.

Through the years they had mutually pushed each other through one challenge after another. They were both presented with their Eagle Scout ranks at the same time. After that they continued to learn new skills—skiing, playing the guitar, cross-country running, playing baseball, fly fishing, and, just before Kyle had left, rock climbing.

On many Friday afternoons in the summer, Jed and Kyle drove into the mountains and camped—spending time hiking, fishing, or climbing the sheer granite spires near where they camped. By Saturday night they were packed again and heading toward home so they could carry out priesthood responsibilities on Sunday.

If it hadn't been for Jed, I'd never have become an Eagle Scout, or even done much at all, Kyle thought as he rolled out of his sleeping bag and crawled over to his suitcase. Rummaging through it, he found his warm-up suit, socks, and tennis shoes, which he put on. He padded quietly through the house, being careful not to disturb his parents and two younger brothers.

Sitting on the front steps, he studied the neighborhood for the first time in daylight. After a few minutes he discovered what was troubling him about the houses in the development. Of the hundreds of homes that stood along the curving suburban street, there were only four basic floor plans. Every fifth house was exactly like the one his family would be living in.

He jogged along the sidewalk for three blocks and then continued down a boulevard, passing small shops and gas stations, some of which were just opening for their Saturday business. The high humidity was like a clammy blanket on his arms and face, causing small beads of sweat to collect.

The large high school complex loomed in front of him on the boulevard a block away. His father had pointed it out as they had passed the night before.

"This is where you'll be going to school." He remembered his father's voice the night before as he now walked around the building. His father didn't seem to understand how hard it was for him to move. "I know you think you're leaving everything behind," his father had said. "But you'll make new friends in Illinois."

Finally Kyle made his way to the oval track that circled the football field. He had run a mile and a half when she appeared. He could hear someone approaching, and then she passed him, a flash of red jogging suit and a bobbing ponytail that progressively left him. He checked his watch to make sure he was maintaining his pace for four miles.

Half a lap later she stopped and began to walk. He caught up with her and passed. A little later she again fired past him and then resumed walking. He decided to quicken his pace. When he reached her, he was running much faster. He passed her as she walked, smiling to himself, confident that a girl didn't have enough endurance to catch him.

A quarter of a lap later, she edged past him. He pushed himself harder, unwilling to let a girl pass him. They continued side by side for a quarter of a lap. Then she eased away from him, sprinting the last half lap before she stopped and continued walking. When he caught up with her, he also stopped to walk.

"You run good—for a girl," he said.

It was apparent she didn't consider that a compliment.

"Oh?" she said, moving loose strands of hair from off

her face. "You run okay—for a boy. Slow but sure, right?"

With that dig, she took off, smoking the track for half a lap before heading away from the school.

The next day was Sunday. Before Sunday School classes began, the Sunday School president came over to Kyle's family and helped direct them to the right rooms. Kyle's younger brothers were helped first. Then the man called across the hall, "Jenny, can you come here?"

Kyle turned to see the girl from the track. They were introduced, and she was asked to show him where her class met. "This will almost double your class size, won't it?" the president asked as they left to find the room.

"It seems like I'm always following you, doesn't it?" Kyle joked as she led the way.

She turned and smiled. "I'm sorry for being so rude yesterday. I've worked hard on running, and I guess I can't joke about it."

The class that day consisted of Jenny, Kyle, and a boy who was visiting from another ward. The teacher, Sister Mattson, seemed to Kyle to be at least sixty years old. She was a convert of six months and was a little hard of hearing. She read much of the lesson from the manual. Kyle sullenly compared her to the teacher in his old ward, who was so well prepared he never even brought the manual to class. *What can she teach me?* he thought, scrunching down in his chair so he could look at the floor and think about his friends back home.

On Monday morning Kyle reported to the school office and registered for classes. He finally left the office during the class change. The endless hall, like some living organism, accepted the bumping, swaying mass of students and then gradually ejected them into different rooms.

Since it was near the beginning of the school year, only the second week of classes, his teachers didn't make much of a fuss over him. He sat unknown in his first two classes.

When the bell rang, old friends joined up, leaving him alone and ignored.

His 11:00 class was sociology. It took him a long time to find the room, so by the time he arrived it was already nearly full. He found an empty desk and sat down.

To his left a boy was scanning a "men's" magazine. As he slowly turned each page on his desk, he grinned, chattering a stream of crude remarks to his friend in front of him.

Kyle looked away to avoid seeing the picture spread blatantly on the desk next to his. He felt his stomach churning; he clenched his teeth tightly thinking sarcastically that he wished his father were there to see some of the friends he was making in his new school.

"Hey, are you new here?" Kyle turned back and saw the boy facing him, holding the rolled-up magazine in one hand. Nodding his head, he said, "Yeah, we just moved here."

"Great. They call me Fitzie," he said, flashing a broad grin. "Hey, have you seen this issue yet? Go ahead, take a look." He plopped the magazine on Kyle's desk. Kyle's mind raced, his internal defense and prosecution lawyers giving their arguments why he should or should not open the magazine to avoid offending the only person who had made any attempt to be a friend.

"C'mon, hurry up," the boy said impatiently. "Class is going to start in a minute. You do want to look at this, don't you?"

Kyle paused for what seemed a long time, then with a smile handed the magazine back. "Later. There's not enough time now."

At first he thought it had been a victory. *After all,* he thought, *I didn't look at the magazine.* But a gnawing uneasiness bothered him.

The class began with Mr. Martin yelling to get everybody to quiet down. Mr. Martin had the voice and face of a movie gangster, but either because of that or in spite of it, he had control and the interest of his class. "Today," he said, leaning against the front of his desk, "we're going to talk about what ethical basis you use in making decisions or why you do the things you do. Fitzie, you usually have something interesting to say. Why do you do some things but don't do others?"

Fitzie extended his feet further into the aisle, attempting to look more relaxed than he was. "I don't know. I'm no philosopher. I just do things."

"But how do you decide?"

"Well," he said with a mischievous grin, "if it looks like fun, then I do it." This brought catcalls of approval from many in the class.

"Darla, what basis do you use in making decisions?" Mr. Martin asked.

Darla sat three seats from Kyle. He was fascinated by her. Her high cheekbones made her look as if some sculptor had fashioned her face. She caught him staring at her and cast him a hurried smile. "I think it's important to be sincere," she answered. "We live in an age of freedom, don't we? All the old barriers are down. We're free to do anything we want to, as long as it doesn't hurt anyone. So all we have to do is to be honest with our feelings."

The discussion came around to dating. Darla raised her hand and Mr. Martin called on her. "If a girl is going with a guy," she said, nervously tapping her pencil on the desk, "and if she really cares about him, and if he's sincerely interested in her at the time, then I think it's okay for them to use their freedom. I mean, what good is freedom if you don't use it?"

Mr. Martin walked across the room toward Darla. "You say if he's sincere at the time. What happens when he no longer cares about her?"

Kyle sat close enough to see her eyes close momentarily,

as if Mr. Martin had found a weakness. She fought for composure for only a moment, her distress unnoticed by most in the class. "Well, of course, people change . . . and drift apart. Maybe if they can just try to be honest with their feelings," her voice trailed off, "while they're together, maybe that's all any of us can hope for."

As the discussion continued, Kyle suddenly realized that he was waiting for someone to stand and present arguments against the ideas being given for doing whatever looked like fun—someone who would say that freedom requires responsibility. In his classes back home in his old high school, although there had been the same reasons given for freedom to "love," there had always been some of his friends who had defended the standards of the gospel.

By the end of the class he realized that the someone he waited for wasn't around anymore. More painful to him, he realized that he had not been that someone.

After class Kyle met with Mr. Martin, who gave him some previous assignments to catch up on. As he turned to leave, Darla was waiting for him. "You're new here, aren't you? Can I show you how to make it through the cafeteria alive?"

They jostled their way through the line and ate by themselves at one end of a table in the corner. While they ate, other boys came and talked with Darla. As they were leaving the cafeteria, she told him, "I'm not going with anyone now . . . in case you were wondering."

They walked outside to the parking lot in back of school. It was filled with students lounging in cars or standing around talking. "You can get anything here in the parking lot if you need it," she said to him.

He looked at her with a puzzled expression.

"You know? Beer, grass, whatever you need."

"Oh," he said, looking more carefully at the cars filled with students.

"Mostly I've given it up. Now it's just for special occasions. How about you?"

"I've never tried it."

"Never? Why not?"

"I don't know," he said weakly, again feeling his stomach tighten up.

"Well, you should," she said, touching his arm, "just to see what it's like. It's fun. Sometime, when my parents are out of town, I'll let you know. Maybe we could get a few others together and have a party."

As he approached the house after school, he could see by the empty boxes near the side door that the moving van had arrived. He walked through the door, made his way past several boxes in the hallway, said hello to his mother, and asked if he could rest a few minutes before helping her unpack.

After shifting a few boxes from the floor of his room, he collapsed on his sleeping bag, bringing the cover to his face to bring back the smell of the last camping trip in the mountains with Jed. They had fished during the days. The snow still hung in drifts in some shady hillsides even then, and they could catch a fish and toss it a few feet onto a snow bank to keep it fresh. He remembered talking with Jed about girls they dated. But those girls were different, he thought. It was just understoood that they lived gospel standards. A few minutes later he forced himself up and went to help his mother.

At six o'clock the family crowded around the kitchen table, stumbling over boxes to get there. They had peanut butter and jelly sandwiches and milk for supper. "How did school go today?" his mother asked. His two younger brothers fought to tell their adventures in grade school.

"Kyle, did you find your way around okay today?" his father asked.

"Yeah," Kyle said, not knowing how he could explain.

"Now tonight," his mother announced, "we'll need everybody to work at unpacking. Let's get going so we can get done."

Kyle was assigned to unpack boxes of books for their new bookshelf. To relieve the boredom of the job, he turned on his portable radio. As he worked, he found himself listening, not just to the music, but to the words of the songs. One song fascinated him. It was sung by a woman. Partway through, he realized he was picturing Darla singing the words to him. The music was soft, the melody haunting, the guitar background skillfully done; but the words were wrong—wrong, at least, compared to what he had been taught in church. He felt the battle within him becoming more fierce. Finally he jumped up and turned the radio off.

In his second week of school, Kyle decided to go out for the cross-country team, partly because he had run for his high school team back home, and partly because Fitzie was the equipment manager of the team and talked him into it.

After Kyle's first practice, the coach told him he was welcome to be on the team. He took his shower and got dressed. Fitzie was standing, holding a bag of practice uniforms that needed laundering, and talking to the others on the team. "Let me tell you a story I heard the other day," Fitzie began. Kyle grabbed his brush and retreated to where there was a mirror in order to get away from hearing the joke. At the punch line the others roared their approval.

Kyle finished with his hair and then returned to his locker. The others had left, and Fitzie was finishing up his work. "Hey, did you hear the joke I was telling a few minutes ago? This will kill you. It seems that there was this guy . . . "

Kyle stood mutely listening to the story, the fight within him erupting again. He hoped it would be over soon, and that it wouldn't be too dirty, and that it would wash away from his memory.

Fitzie finished the joke. "How about that, huh? It's sort of a cute story, isn't it? Darla told me that the other day. Well, I've got to be going."

Kyle sat down on the bench in front of his locker and stared numbly at the floor for a long time. He felt that he was losing his battle with his thoughts. Suddenly he stood up and put on his running uniform and shoes. Coach Schmidt came out of his office on the way home just as Kyle was heading for the track. "Are you still here?"

"I'm going to run some more," Kyle said deliberately.

"Five miles isn't enough for one day?"

"Is it okay? Will I still be able to get into the gym when I'm through?"

"Sure," the coach said, heading for the door. "It's open until nine."

On the track Kyle forced himself to maintain a fast pace, trying to push all the debris in his mind out with the sweat, hoping to somehow cleanse himself from his thoughts.

After three laps Jenny appeared alongside him, going at his pace. "What are you doing here?" he asked as they ran side by side.

"I always run after school. Do you think you can keep up with me today?"

They ran for two miles, and then Kyle stopped. "I thought you might be getting tired. That's why I stopped," he explained as they walked around the track.

"Me tired?" she smiled, teasing him, "at this slow pace? You didn't need to stop for me. I can run at this pace for hours."

"Oh, yeah, then why don't you go out for cross-country?"

"Because," she said, wiping her forehead, "I'm a sprinter. I run the 100, the 220, and the 440 in track. I've won some races too. Have you ever won a race?"

"Sure, back home."

"Well, this isn't there."

"I'm finding that out," he said, feeling the oppressive gloom settling on his mind again. They walked silently for a while. Then he asked, "Jenny, how do you survive here?"

"What do you mean?"

"Everything. The way everybody jokes about the wrong things. Everyone seems willing to do anything that looks like fun."

"Not everyone," Jenny said. "You just have to be careful who your friends are. I've got some really good friends who aren't LDS, but they keep their standards high."

"Well, everyone I've met acts like they've never even heard the word *chastity*. Things are different back where I came from. I have a friend there—Jed. He always lives the standards, but he's fun to be around, too. He's always looking for new adventures. We climbed some granite cliffs this summer . . . "

"Kyle, you can't keep living back there. You're here now, remember? I don't know what it was like back there, but you're wrong about the kids here. You could meet some of my friends instead of going around with Fitzie . . . and Darla."

He felt his face getting red.

"Why do you eat lunch with her?" Jenny asked.

"Because she's the only one who's made any real effort to be a friend," he said, feeling his voice tense up.

"Watch out for her."

"I thought we weren't supposed to judge people," he snapped.

"Okay, I'm sorry. But look, you can rationalize all you want about how wicked it is here and how great it was there, but you'd better face the fact that you chose your friends back there, and you're choosing your friends here. It's *your* choice. Don't put the blame on the place. Put it on yourself where it belongs."

They had stopped walking and were squared off at each other. "You're jealous," he accused.

"What do you want? An excuse to get involved with her so that if you mess up your life, you can always say that things are rotten here so how could you help making a mistake? Is that what you want? An excuse?"

He wanted to get away from her, to leave her standing on the track, never to have to face her question. He turned and began walking away. She caught up with him and walked beside him. They didn't say anything for a lap. Then she said quietly, "Kyle, I'm not your enemy. I want to be your friend. Okay?"

He didn't say anything for a while. His first words came out weak and uncertain. "Darla is the most beautiful girl I've ever known."

"I know," Jenny said quietly.

After that he ran with Jenny every day after he finished his workout with the team. A week later, after they had finished and were walking together, he again confided in her. "Darla's invited me to a party at her house a week from Saturday."

"Are you going?" Jenny asked.

"I don't know. Part of me says yes—it will be fun. Another part says that I shouldn't go. I guess whatever part is stronger will decide."

"Kyle," she said, touching his arm, "don't go. It won't be any good for you."

"I know. But what if I don't go . . . this time?" he agonized. "What about the next time she asks me? What will I say then? When will I break down and go? How long will it be before this place breaks me down? I want to go back to my friends back home."

"Have you prayed about this? I mean really prayed about your problems?"

He shook his head and confessed, "I haven't felt worthy to pray."

"That's the time you need to pray the most," she said.

That night he had a dream. In his dream he was fishing from a boat with Jed as they had done many times. It was the same lake in the mountains that they had been to that summer. At first he was catching fish, laughing with Jed, having a good time. Then the dream changed, and he was alone in the boat. The boat was leaking, and all he had to bail it out with was a plastic drinking cup. At first he was able to stay ahead of the water, but then it got worse. He bailed furiously to keep the boat from sinking, but he could see the water filling the boat. When he looked up, he saw Darla and Fitzie on the shore laughing at him, yelling for him to let the boat sink.

Suddenly he wrenched free of his dream. He was sweating, and his covers were in disarray. He got out of bed, turned on his light, and looked at the time. It was twelve-thirty.

He lay down, and tried to go back to sleep, but sleep wouldn't come. All the offending thoughts poured down upon his mind in rapid succession. He threw back the covers and got out of bed. Putting on a pair of slacks and a shirt, he walked outside onto the front steps and sat down. The sky was free of clouds, and he could see the stars clearly. He found himself identifying some of the constellations that he had learned in Scouting.

Sitting there, he relived in his mind what Jed and he had gone through in order to earn their Eagle Scout ranks. He remembered how Jed was always in front, leading the way. Suddenly he found an answer to his problems: "I'll call Jed and ask if I can move in with his family!" His mind raced, picturing himself back again with his friends.

He hurried inside and went into the family room where there was an extension phone. He dialed Jed's number.

The sleepy voice of Jed's mother answered the phone. He apologized for calling so late and asked if he could talk to Jed.

Jed answered the phone, and they talked for a few minutes about small things. Then Jed asked, "Is anything wrong?"

"I want to move back there. Do you think your parents will let me move in with your family? I could get a job and pay them for room and board. My parents would probably help too."

"I'll ask them in the morning," Jed answered. "What's wrong?"

"I don't like it here. The people are really different." He told Jed about the drugs and loose morals, painting it in as bad a light as he could.

Jed was unimpressed. "So what? I can find the same attitudes back here in our high school. Have you forgotten?"

Kyle felt as if his last hope was being yanked away. "No! It's different. I've got to get out of here, or I'll end up being just like them."

"Why don't you try to set a good example?" Jed asked.

"I can't. They'll laugh at me. Let me come back."

"Okay, if you need to, we'll work it out. But Kyle, maybe you've got some missionary work you can do there."

"No, not me. How can I convert them? They've nearly converted me."

"Look," Jed continued, "since we were in grade school, you've been somebody I've looked to for help. You practically dragged me through to become an Eagle. You were always the one who was out ahead yelling for us to catch up."

Kyle was stunned to hear Jed say that. "No, not me. You were the leader."

"I had to hustle to stay up with you," Jed insisted. "Didn't you know that? Now find some friends there who will lift you up the way we helped each other."

Kyle pictured in his mind the way the halls overflowed during a class change. "How will I find them? There are two thousand kids in the school."

"I don't know. You'll find a way. You always have before when you faced a challenge."

They said good-bye, and Kyle hung up. He walked slowly to his room, lost in thought. Kneeling by his bed, he began a long prayer: "Father in heaven, I've got a problem . . . "

The next night after supper he went with Fitzie and some of his friends to play basketball in the school gym. They played for two hours. Afterward they were all in the locker room. Kyle had already showered and was just putting on his shoes. The others were in various stages of getting dressed. Suddenly the lights went out. "Okay, who's the clown?" Fitzie yelled. "Turn the lights back on!"

"I didn't turn 'em off," someone answered. "Where's the light switch anyway? . . . Ow! My toe! . . . The switch doesn't work."

"There aren't any lights anywhere in the building," another voice added.

"Oh, no," Fitzie groaned, "another blackout. Do any of you guys have a lighter?"

"I do," someone volunteered. "It's in my shirt pocket, if I can find it." Kyle could make out a figure fumbling in a locker near him. "Here it is."

A small glimmer of light shone in the otherwise dark room. "Hurry up, you guys! I'm low on lighter fluid."

Kyle sat on the bench and watched unknown figures make use of the small light as they finished preparing to leave the room.

"Man, I never thought I'd be glad somebody had a cheap lighter," a voice drawled.

"What do you mean, cheap lighter? It cost me two bucks."

"Yeah, well it sure seems bright in here."

Finally they were ready. "Kyle, what are you doing sitting there? Let's go."

On Sunday Kyle went with Jenny to class, mainly to

be with her. He had already discounted any possibility that their teacher could teach him anything, so he sat with his shoulders hunched over, his head down, wrestling with his problems.

It wasn't until Sister Mattson called on him that he looked up. "Kyle," she said, then read aloud from the manual, "this can best be seen by examining what the Savior said. Will you read Matthew, chapter 5, verses 14 through 16?"

Jenny loaned him her Bible and helped him find the reference. " 'Ye are the light of the world,' " Kyle began mechanically. " 'A city that is set on an hill cannot be hid. Neither do men light a candle, and put it under a bushel, but on a candlestick; and it giveth light . . . ' " He stopped and stared at the words on the page.

"Yes, go on," Sister Mattson urged.

" ' . . . and it giveth light unto all that are in the house.' "

"Kyle, there's one more verse," Jenny quietly prompted.

" 'Let your light so shine before men,' " he read slowly, " 'that they may see your good works, and glorify your Father which is in heaven.' "

"Yes, and what can we learn from this scripture?" Sister Mattson asked.

He didn't say anything. He pictured the small light in the darkened locker room and the dim figures of people moving around, each attracted by the light and using it as their reference point.

"Jenny, do you know what we can learn from this scripture?" Sister Mattson asked, thinking that Kyle did not have an answer.

"We can learn a lot," Kyle said quietly, almost to himself. "The first thing is that in order to be a light, we have to live the commandments. You have to set your standards. You can't re-decide what to do every time someone asks you to do something wrong. You've got to make a mental list: This is what I will do. This is what I won't do. You have to decide what your life is going to mean, or it won't mean a thing."

"Thank you," Sister Mattson said. "Now we should get on with the rest of the lesson."

Kyle interrupted. "The problem is, I keep thinking that if I didn't live here, it would be easier. It doesn't really matter where you live. What matters is that you set your standards once and for all. If you do that, you can be a light."

"Yes, thank you, and now we'd better get on to Ephesians," Sister Mattson said.

"You've got to be a light to the people around you. Do you know how much light one small lighter can throw in a completely dark room?"

"No," Jenny replied.

"Enough. That's the point. Enough for everyone in the room to find his way out of the darkness. And the darker it is, the more the light is noticed. And people who enjoy the light will come nearer to it. That's how I can find friends who will help me live my standards! We can gather friends around us who will help us, and the light will get even brighter."

Sister Mattson by now was just looking at both of them.

"Do you know what I'm going to do?" Kyle burst out. "I'm going to memorize jokes from my brother's *Boy's Life* magazine. It has some of the corniest jokes in the world. Every time I hear someone starting a dirty joke, I'm going to bombard him with corny jokes. And I'm going to have a party of my own, at my house, with kids from school and the missionaries. In a nice friendly way, they're going to know I'm a Mormon."

"Thank you, Kyle," Sister Mattson broke in. Turning to Jenny, she asked confidentially, "Jenny, what did he say?"

Jenny put her hand on his arm and answered proudly, "He said that he's going to be okay."

"How nice," Sister Mattson said. "Well, we'd better get on with the rest of the lesson." She looked at the page of the manual, paused, and then shut the book. "No, I think Kyle's story can teach us the same thing. What were you saying about the light in the dark room?"

The Greatest Game Ever

It was during the fourth quarter of the Division II semifinal game that Western Ohio University's star quarterback Chad Halliday was injured. A day later as the team left for California to prepare for the national championship game, Chad was left behind, still laid up in the hospital.

Being in the hospital was nearly unbearable for Chad. Besides being angry at not getting to play in the championship game, he had nothing to do to occupy his time. By the first day he'd already watched enough TV to last him a lifetime. He found himself looking forward to the butterscotch pudding they served for supper—it was the highlight of his day.

The day after the team left, a nurse he'd never seen before entered his room. Chad decided that either she was the most beautiful woman in the world or he had already lost his mind to boredom. In either case his imagination raced ahead of reality. He pictured the two of them spending every waking moment together, sharing candlelight suppers in his hospital room, walking hand in hand down the deserted corridors late at night. And when it came time for him to leave, they would linger at the hospital door, both of them wishing it didn't have to end.

These were his fantasies as she entered his room. But

life is often cruel. "Good morning," she said, "it's time for your shot. Turn over, please."

He began to blush. "Uh . . . can we talk about this?"

"Is something wrong?"

"It's just that . . . uh . . . I feel great. There's no need for you to give me a shot. Really, it'd just be a waste."

"I give dozens of shots every day. It's nothing to be embarrassed about."

"That's easy for you to say. You're not the one who has to turn over. By the way, what's your name?"

"Jaymie London."

"Nice to meet you, although not this way, of course. I'm Chad Halliday. I'm Western Ohio's quarterback. I led our team to an 8 and 1 season. Two weeks ago my picture was in *Sports Illustrated* as one of the leading passers for small colleges. Even though I'm active in sports, I've managed to maintain a 3.1 grade point average . . . "

She smiled. "You're not stalling, are you?"

"Me? Stalling? What gives you that idea?"

"Because you haven't turned over yet."

"Look, there's no way I'm going to turn over. Give me the shot in the arm."

"It'll hurt worse there."

He shrugged. "I'm a quarterback—I'm used to pain."

"All right. Which arm?"

"My left arm. I throw with my right. Two hundred and thirty-seven yards last game, until I got hurt, but, hey, I don't expect sympathy." He was fishing, but it got him nowhere.

"Left arm it is," she said. She made preparations to give the shot.

"Jaymie, how about stopping by after work? I'll phone in an order of pizza, we'll have a few laughs and get acquainted. Whataya say?"

"No thanks." She gave him the shot. "There," she said. "I hope that's not too painful."

His arm was killing him, but there was no way he was going to admit it. He smiled. "No problem. By the way, did you happen to go to any home games this year?"

"No."

"Since you're not a football fan, let me explain something. In this town I'm kind of a sports hero."

"Yes. So?"

"So women don't usually turn me down when I ask 'em out."

"That must work out great for you then, right? Well, I've got to run."

"Look, I don't need you. There's plenty of women in this town who'd love to spend time with me."

"Oh? Where are they now?"

His shoulders slumped. "I don't know. Busy, I guess."

"You poor guy. How about if I put up a notice on the nurses' bulletin board? There must be somebody around here who'd be interested."

"Look, just forget it, okay? I don't need your help. Really. Lots of women love me."

"Good. That means you don't need me. See you around."

He called out as she was leaving, "You're not fooling me. I'm on to your little game."

She turned to look at him. "What little game?"

"You've figured out how much I thrive on competition. That's why you're playing hard to get."

She smiled. "I'm not playing hard to get—I *am* hard to get. Well, I gotta go." And with that she left him.

The last time a girl had turned Chad down for a date had been when he was a sophomore in high school. That was just before his first football game, a game that changed his entire life. It being his first year on the team, he was the second-string quarterback. But by the fourth quarter, they were behind twenty points, so the coach put Chad in just to give him some playing time. But Chad thought he was supposed to win the game. And so he did. He threw four touchdown passes. After that he had no trouble getting dates with any girl he wanted. Until now. He decided he'd just have to work harder. The next time she came in, he was ready for her.

"What's that weird smell?" she asked, turning up her nose.

"It's my after-shave. It's called Macho Musk. It's made from the musk oil of a male deer. It's supposed to be very appealing."

She sniffed. "To another deer, maybe."

"All right, forget the after-shave. You're sure you won't come see me after work?"

"Positive."

He swallowed the two pills she gave him. "You're the stubbornest girl I've ever met."

"Just because I'm not telling you how wonderful you are? That's not stubbornness, that's good judgment."

"How about if I phone you tonight?"

"Look, it's been fun to kid around with you, but the fact is I'm a health-care professional and you're one of my patients. I'm not in this job to meet guys, okay? So don't phone me after work."

"Forget we're in a hospital. Suppose you were at the library on campus and I walked in and sat down and we started talking and I asked you out. Would you go out with me then?"

"Probably not."

"Good grief, lady, what's your problem? Are you intimidated being around a real man?"

"Gosh, I don't know. Are you a real man?"

"You bet I am."

She snickered. "Then I guess I'm not intimidated."

"C'mon, Jaymie, why won't you go out with me?"

She paused. "The main reason is because I'm a Mormon."

"I don't care. I still want to go out with you."

"I don't date guys who aren't Mormon."

"Hey, no problem. I'll join. Is there a card I sign or what?"

"It's not that simple."

"Why not?"

"Look, I have to go now."

"Come back and tell me about your church."

"You're not interested in my church."

"You don't know that for sure. The least you can do is come and tell me about it."

She sighed. "All right, I'll come back when I have my break."

After she left, he phoned down to the gift shop and ordered an expensive lounging robe and had it delivered. When she returned, he was sitting on the bed in his robe. She took one look at him and burst out laughing.

"What's so funny?" he asked.

"You look like you stepped out of one of those English murder mysteries where they have everybody meet in the drawing room to find out who the murderer is."

"Hey, this cost a lot of money. I can't please you, can I?"

"No, don't even try. Look, I can't stay long. You said you wanted to know about my church. All right, I'll tell you about it. The most important thing is that we're Christian, so we believe in the Bible like other churches, but we have other things that no other church has. We have a prophet of God, and additional scripture, and the priesthood . . . "

"Hey, can we skip the theology lesson? I just want to know how to join."

"You can't skip the doctrine. It makes everything else fit together."

"Then do it another time. For now, just tell me how to join."

"All right. There are certain standards you'd be expected to keep."

"Like what?"

"Well, honesty, for example."

"No problem."

"And Mormons don't use alcohol."

"Wait a minute, let's go back—we just glossed over honesty. I don't think you appreciate how honest I really am."

She smiled. "I take it you drink."

He shrugged his shoulders. "A few beers once in a while. That's all."

"How often?"

"Well, if we win a game . . . or if we lose a game . . . if I flunk a test . . . or if I do really well on it." He paused. "Sounds like I'm a real lush, doesn't it? I'm not. I can quit anytime. What else?"

"No coffee or tea or tobacco."

"I never use tea or tobacco. Coffee might be a problem, though. I use it to sober up after . . . never mind. What else?"

"Mormons believe in chastity. That means before marriage nothing goes."

"Nothing?" he asked.

"Nothing."

There was a long silence. She was looking at him strangely.

"It's not that I've lived such a wild life," he said. "It's just that I didn't know anybody still felt that way about morality."

"I've stayed morally clean all my life, and that's what I expect from my future husband."

He sighed. "This is kind of a hard church to belong to, isn't it? What else?"

"You'd be asked to pay tithing. That's ten percent of your income."

"How about if I just donate a couple dollars every week?"

"Tithing means ten percent. Another thing—you'd be expected to go to church every Sunday and maybe even teach a Sunday School class." She paused. "Still interested?"

He sighed. "Maybe you're right. Maybe we should've started with the doctrine."

"Yeah, I think so. It's not as hard to live as it sounds, if you believe the church is true."

"Suppose I did join. Would you go out with me then?"

"Probably not."

"Why not?"

She paused. "Because I'm waiting for a missionary."

"What does that mean?"

"When a Mormon guy turns nineteen, he spends two years at his own expense telling people about the church. The guy I'm waiting for is named Everett Larson. I met him last year. Now he's on a mission in New Mexico."

"He's probably out there dating all the local girls."

"Missionaries don't date."

"What do you mean, they don't date? They're single?"

"Yes."

"And they're . . . uh . . . healthy?"

"Sure."

"Are they normal?"

She smiled. "Very normal."

"You expect me to believe normal, healthy guys don't date for two years?"

"That's right."

"Who'd ever agree to that? How many missionaries are there? Ten? Twenty? A hundred?"

"Thirty-two thousand."

"How can that be? I couldn't go two weeks without a date. How can anyone go two years?"

"They've dedicated themselves to the Lord."

"And they pay their own way?"

"Either that or their parents help out."

He thought about it for a long time and then said quietly, "That's unreal." He looked up at her. "If I were a member, would you be encouraging me to go on a mission?"

"Yes. It'd be the best thing you could do."

"Even better than playing football in the NFL?"

"Yes, even better than that."

"That shows how little you know about football."

"No, what it shows is how little you know about the gospel of Jesus Christ."

"Someday millions of people will be watching me play in the Super Bowl."

"All right, that may happen. But you can't play professional football forever. What happens when the crowds stop cheering and you're left all alone? What will you do then?"

He smiled faintly. "I'll do beer commercials."

"There's more to life than that." She paused. "Look, there's something I haven't told you. There's a book I want you to read. It's called the Book of Mormon. If I bring you a copy, will you read it?"

"I might." He looked at her. "Jaymie, do you and I have any kind of a future?"

"No," she said softly.

"Not even for a couple of days?"

"No."

"Look, if you come by to see me tonight after you get off work, there's no way this missionary of yours will ever know about it. I mean, you could trust me not to say a word to anyone."

"Sorry. I guess I'm just a one-man woman."

He sighed. "Maybe you'd better put that notice up on the nurses' bulletin board after all."

"Whatever you say."

"Just kidding. I do okay by myself."

That night he phoned a sorority and asked them to send some girls over to cheer him up. Fifteen came. They stayed way past visiting hours. The head nurse, a crusty woman named Gortman, personally escorted them out of the building three times, but each time they sneaked up the stairs and into Chad's room when nobody was looking. Things were pretty much out of control until one o'clock in the morning when Gortman called the police.

The next morning when Jaymie came into Chad's room, he could tell she'd been told what went on the night before.

"Where do you want your shot today?" she said icily.

"My right arm."

"Really? How are you ever going to hug all your female admirers with your best arm out of commission?"

"It wasn't as bad as people make it sound."

"Are you telling me you didn't lead a parade of girls down the hall at midnight?"

"All right, that happened, but we were very quiet."

"And you didn't have the girls try to sneak you out of the hospital so you could all go out for pizza?"

"Yeah, well, we tried it, but we got caught when they tried to roll my bed into the freight elevator. But hey, we didn't bother any of the other patients. Besides, it gave Gorbachev or whatever your head nurse is called something to do all night instead of falling asleep at the desk."

She pointed her finger at him. "Let me tell you something, Mr. Football Hero. I'm sure you think what you did last night was really cute, but I resent you treating this hospital like it was your own private circus."

Chad wanted to change the subject. "You said you were going to bring me a copy of the Book of Mormon. So, where is it?"

"It's in my locker," she grumbled.

"Are you still going to give it to me?"

"Why, do you need it to prop open the exit doors so you can sneak in more girls after visiting hours?"

"Hey, I might even read it. Did you ever think of that?"

She frowned at him. "All right, I'll bring it to you later on."

She dropped it by half an hour later. She had marked some passages in red, and he started on them, but after a few minutes he got bored and put it down and turned on the TV to watch a rerun of "Paradise Island."

That night some girls dropped by, but when visiting hours were over two security guards came and escorted them out of the hospital, warning them that if they came back, they'd be arrested.

Chad spent the rest of the night watching TV.

The next morning Jaymie accompanied two orderlies as they wheeled an old man into Chad's room. "What's going on here?" Chad asked.

"This is Mr. Bellini," Jaymie said. "He'll be staying in here with you for a while."

"There's not supposed to be anyone else in here with me."

"Why's that? The university's not paying for a private room."

"The coach made arrangements that I'd be in here alone."

"Sorry, but this is the flu season and there aren't any other beds available. Don't worry, he won't be here long."

"Why's that?"

"Because he's dying."

"Hey, I don't want some old geezer moaning all night when I'm trying to get some sleep."

"He'll be unconscious most of the time."

"If he's unconscious, then why not put him in the hall? He'd never know the difference, right?"

"We're putting him here," she shot back.

Chad made her pull the curtains around the old man's bed so he didn't have to look at him.

Jaymie was right. The old man wasn't much trouble. Nobody came to visit him, and he slept most of the time. But at two-thirty in the morning, he gained consciousness and started mumbling, "Raymond, Raymond, Raymond . . . "

"Hey, quiet down," Chad sleepily called out.

"Raymond," the old man continued, "you came. I knew you'd come. I brought the scrapbook. I want you to have it. Show it to your grandchildren. Tell them I performed before the Queen of England."

Chad sat up in bed. "Hey, pipe down. I'm trying to sleep."

The old man stopped for a minute but then started in again. Chad grabbed the pillow and wrapped it around his ears so he couldn't hear. Eventually he fell asleep.

When Jaymie came into his room later that morning, Chad was still mad. "Get this geek out of here. All night he was mumbling about somebody named Raymond and some dumb scrapbook."

"The man's dying, Chad. Doesn't that mean anything to you?"

He paused. "It's not contagious, is it?"

"You're hopeless."

"So he's dying. What do you want me to do about it?"

"How about showing a little compassion?" she said.

"Hey, old man," he called out, "I'm sorry you're dying." He turned to Jaymie. "How's that?"

"Where do you want your shot?" she snapped.

He sighed and shrugged his shoulders. "I'm out of arms."

"Turn over, then," she ordered.

He turned over. It seemed to him she must have sunk the needle in clear to its handle.

When he turned around again, she said, "I bet that didn't hurt a brave guy like you, did it?"

So she had hurt him on purpose. He wasn't going to give her any satisfaction. "Hey, I could hardly feel it."

"I can believe that. Seems like a lot of feelings never get through to you, doesn't it?" And with that she left.

She had made Chad feel a little ashamed of the way he'd been acting. A few minutes later he limped slowly to the curtain and opened it and looked in at the old man. He was asleep. His face was chalky white in color and dry and cracked like old leather. For some reason the old man woke up. He looked at Chad and smiled. "Raymond, you came. I knew you'd come. I want you to have the scrapbook. Show it to your kids."

"I'm not Raymond," Chad said softly.

"Take the scrapbook, Raymond."

Chad looked around. "Uh, I don't see it, but I'll check on it for you." He went to the closet and rummaged around. There underneath the man's things was a faded brown scrapbook.

"I found it," he called out to the old man. There was no answer. He limped over and looked at the old man. He was asleep again.

Chad went back to his bed and looked through the scrapbook. Eventually he understood what the pictures meant. Antonio Bellini, as a young man, and his brother, Salvatore, had been trapeze artists. The first few newspaper clippings were in Italian. As he turned one tattered page after another, he saw life pass by for the Bellini Brothers. In time the clippings and old advertising fliers were about their appearances in England.

On another page he found a wedding certificate from England, dated May 3, 1957. Antonio Bellini had married an English girl named Victoria Ashworth. The next page contained a carefully preserved program of a performance for Queen Elizabeth. It was dated July 14, 1958.

Three pages later the clippings started coming from

America. The Bellini Brothers were featured in the Shrine Circus. There was a birth certificate for Raymond Bellini, born January 29, 1960, in Orlando, Florida, to Antonio and Victoria Bellini. Page after page of clippings. Apparently whenever his name had appeared in print, Antonio had pasted it in his scrapbook.

Chad thought about his own scrapbook. At first his mother had kept it, but then after he moved away to college, he had started keeping it himself. He hadn't pasted the most recent newspaper clippings in yet, but he knew that someday he would.

Another news item. In 1968 Antonio's brother was killed in an accident while they were performing in Merced, California. He had fallen and the net had broken. He turned the page. There was an obituary about his wife's death from natural causes. April 3, 1975. There was just one more article, not pasted in yet. It told of Raymond Bellini's conviction for robbing a liquor store. It was dated September 3, 1982.

And that was all there was. Chad stared at the sleeping figure of Antonio Bellini. Where were the cheering crowds now? he wondered. Who would remember the life of Antonio Bellini? The same question came to mind about himself. When his life was over, what would it matter that he'd lived and died, or that he'd been the reason Western Ohio made it to the national championship? Who would care in twenty years? He wanted to talk to Jaymie because he knew she'd have some answers for him. He pushed his call button. The head nurse came. He told her he wanted to talk to Jaymie. She told him Jaymie was busy and that he should quit making such a nuisance of himself.

The afternoon dragged on. He kept reading over the tattered scrapbook, trying to piece together the life of Antonio Bellini.

At four-thirty that afternoon he got a phone call from

one of the coeds at the sorority telling him they'd be over at seven. He realized he'd been so wrapped up in the scrapbook that he'd forgotten the Division II championship game was going to be televised that night.

Before the girls showed up, he met with the head nurse and made arrangements for them to use the nurses' lounge during the game. She was against it at first, but agreed because she knew her boss was a big football fan and would override her decision if she said no.

The girls clustered around Chad, who was sitting in a wheelchair, wearing his lounging robe for their benefit. For Chad, watching the game was like being dead and seeing life go on without him. The quarterback replacing Chad was psyched up for the game. In the first ten minutes of play he threw two touchdown passes. At halftime Western Ohio left the field with a 17-0 lead.

Chad asked one of the girls to take him back to his room. Four volunteered. He let them take turns pushing him. Just before they got to his room he said, "You need to be kind of quiet, Mr. Bellini isn't doing very well. He's dying."

"Weird," one of the girls said.

He turned on the TV in his room and lay in bed to watch. During the second half the opposing team scored twice, each time on a time-consuming running attack. By the beginning of the fourth quarter the game was tied. Then, finally, things seemed to be going the right way. Western Ohio began a drive on their twenty-yard line. Four minutes later they were on their opponents' twelve-yard line with a first and ten.

One of the night nurses came in to check on Mr. Bellini, who had been muttering Raymond's name off and on all night. She turned to Chad and asked, "Do you know who Raymond is?"

"Yeah. It's his son."

"Any chance he'll be coming?"

"I don't think so."

"Too bad. The old man is going fast. Could be any minute."

"I'd better talk to him." Chad stood up.

Antonio Bellini reached out and grabbed Chad's hand and held it tight. "Raymond, you came, I knew you'd come. There's something I have to tell you. It makes no sense what happened between us . . . Raymond . . . you're my son, my flesh and blood . . . "

A girl rushed into the room. "Chad! We did it! We're going to win! Come on, I'll wheel you down so you can celebrate with us. Hurry!" Chad felt the effort it took for Antonio to hold on to his hand, his last effort to tell his son he loved him. Chad couldn't leave now. He shook his head.

A few minutes later the girls came and told him they were leaving to go celebrate.

The night dragged on. The old man drifted in and out of consciousness. At one point he woke up, looked over at Chad, and smiled. "Raymond, I'm glad you came."

"I'm glad too."

"You take the scrapbook. Show it to your grandkids some day."

"I will."

"Tell them their grandfather performed before the Queen of England."

For some reason tears were streaming down Chad's face. "They'll be so proud of you, Dad."

The old man smiled contentedly and closed his eyes to rest.

Chad stayed at his bedside until four in the morning, when Antonio Bellini died. Then he lay on his back on his own bed and thought for a long time.

When Chad woke up at seven that morning Mr. Bellini

was gone. The bed was remade, ready for the next patient.

When Jaymie came into Chad's room that morning, she found him looking out the window, deep in thought.

"Mr. Bellini died last night," he said quietly.

"I know. They told me, and about what you did for him."

"He was a trapeze artist, you know. One time he performed before the Queen of England," he said. "It's all here in his scrapbook. I'm keeping it until I can find his son and tell him what his father said about him just before he died." He paused. "I learned something last night."

"What's that?"

"Youth and strength and football won't last forever."

"No."

"Some things are more important than performing before the Queen of England or winning a championship football game." He paused. "I think I'm ready to learn the doctrine now."

Oh, Susanne, Don't You Cry for Us

A year after Matt's mother died, his father started dating again. Several months later he announced that he had invited Jean, the woman he had been seeing, over to their house for supper.

"What for?" Matt grumbled.

"So you can get to know her."

Matt scowled. "I don't want to know her."

"She's coming anyway, so don't make any plans for Friday night. Oh, one other thing: she has a daughter."

On Friday night Jean Porter and her daughter, Susanne, came over for supper. To Matt the fact that Mrs. Porter was a capable, decent, attractive woman was bad news. He didn't like having his father spend time with her because it seemed disloyal to the memory of his mother.

Susanne was, like Matt, fifteen years old. Matt didn't care for her much because she had a certain niceness that bugged him in girls. For instance, she smiled at nearly anything anyone said. To him she seemed the type who tries to answer every question in Sunday School class.

After supper, Matt's father took them to a video rental place. Because Matt was in a foul mood anyway, he chose a horror movie. As he might have predicted, Susanne picked a musical comedy. To avoid an argument, Matt's father got both. At home his dad started Susanne's movie first. Soon after the movie started, his father and Jean decided to go for a ride. Before they left Matt's father took him aside. "Don't go running off. Susanne's your guest, so stay here with her and watch the movie."

After they left, Matt sat in the half-light of the TV room, as far as he could get from Susanne, while they watched what he considered was the worst movie ever made. After a while he couldn't stand it, so he went to the kitchen and started cleaning up. Ever since his mother had died, it had been his job to do the dishes.

A few minutes later, Susanne came in the kitchen. "Need any help?"

It made him mad that she was trying to be helpful. "No."

"I could dry for you."

"I said I don't need any help, okay?"

"You don't have to be such a grouch."

Matt decided to pop her balloon and bring her down. "What happened to your dad?"

He was right; that stopped her. Her face clouded over. "My parents got a divorce. My dad got involved with a woman at work. Her name is Estelle. He got excommunicated from the church. My mother divorced him and then he married Estelle." She paused. "It was a bad deal. What happened to your mother?"

"She was in a car crash and died."

"I'm sorry."

"Yeah, right."

"I bet you miss her a lot."

Matt didn't want her to say all those things people say to try to make you feel better. He'd heard it all before and it hadn't made him feel better. "Look, go watch your movie, okay?"

She shrugged her shoulders and left.

He finished the dishes. He couldn't watch TV because that was what she was doing, so he went in his room and listened to music on his stereo. Until she knocked on his door.

"What?" he called out, turning down the radio.

"I need to talk to you. It's important."

He opened the door. She looked inside. "Is this your bedroom?"

"No, it's a walk-in freezer," he grumbled.

"What are the trophies for?"

"I was on a swim team."

"Why aren't you now?"

"They practiced at five in the morning. My mom used to take me and wait for the practice to be over."

"But now that your mother's gone, you don't go anymore."

"My mother's not gone, she's dead," Matt snapped.

"I know that."

"Then why did you say *gone*? Were you trying to spare me? Well, forget it. What did you need to talk to me about, anyway?"

"You don't like me, do you?"

"Did I say that? Besides, what does it matter? We'll never see each other again anyway."

"Don't count on it."

"What do you mean?"

"That's what I wanted to talk to you about. Has your dad talked at all about my mom?"

"No."

"He will."

"How do you know?"

"I heard them talking last night. They're planning on getting married. They want us to get used to each other before they tell us."

"You're lying. My dad would never get married again."

"Look, I'm not making this up. It's going to happen, and there's nothing we can do to stop it. So we might as well get used to the idea."

"My dad loved my mom too much to ever get married again. So get out and quit sticking your nose in other people's business."

"All right, but don't say I didn't warn you." She returned to the TV room.

Matt went in the living room and paced the floor, waiting for his father and Jean to come back. As soon as they walked in, he hit them with it. "Susanne says you're thinking about getting married. That's not true, is it?"

His father cleared his throat. "Well, uh, this is sooner than we had planned to talk about it, but as long as you brought it up, how would you feel about that?"

"We don't need her, Dad. We can get along fine without anyone else."

"Matt," his father began. "Someday you'll understand how it's been for me with your mother gone . . . "

"You mean it's true?"

"Yes, it's true. Jean and I want very much to get married."

"Well, what are we supposed to do about Mom, just forget she ever existed?"

"No, of course not," his dad answered.

"Matt, look, I know this is a shock," Jean said, "and I promise there'll be no marriage until you and Susanne both feel good about it. Your dad and I want to get married in the temple, and we'd very much like you and Susanne to be waiting for us together when we come out." She paused. "But we can't go to the temple if there are any bad feelings between any of us."

"Good, that means it'll never happen," Matt snapped, storming off to his room and slamming the door.

Later that night, after Jean and Susanne had left, his father knocked on his door. Matt let him in.

"I think we should talk," his father said.

"What's there to talk about? You've already decided what you're going to do. You're going to bring that woman and her smiley-faced daughter into this home. I can stand it without a mother. Why can't you stand it without a wife?"

"Matt, part of the reason I'm doing this is for you."

"Oh, sure," Matt grumbled.

"It's true. Women bring joy into a home. Like your mother did for us. You remember what it was like coming home when she'd just baked some cookies. Or when you had a report to do in school, how she helped you. Or when you became a deacon, how proud she was to have you give her the sacrament. Remember when I got that promotion? The first thing I did was to tell your mother the good news because I knew she'd give that little victory shout she always did, and that was better than the promotion. Well, we need that again in our home. I can't bring it and you can't either. It takes a woman to make things better. Once you get to know Jean, you'll see what a wonderful person she is." He paused. "Next Saturday we're going cross-country skiing."

"With them?"

"Yes."

"Do I have to go?"

"Yes."

On Saturday morning they picked up Jean and Susanne in their four-wheel drive station wagon and took off for the mountains. Matt and Susanne sat in the back seat, as far apart as possible, both of them silent and staring out their windows, while his dad and Jean were in the front, providing most of the conversation.

There was a cross-country trail in the mountains that went on for miles. It had once been a railroad bed, but when the railroad went bankrupt, the rails and wooden ties were sold for scrap. Eventually the state bought the right-of-way and turned it into a cross-country trail.

It was Jean's first time cross-country skiing, so she couldn't keep up with everybody else. Matt's father stayed behind and helped her.

Matt had planned on ditching Susanne, but she had gone skiing before and she was surprisingly strong. No matter how much he pushed, she managed to keep up with him. Soon there was silence except for the sound of their skis sliding over the cold snow and the sound of their breathing as they made the steady climb up along the trail.

Half an hour after they'd started, Susanne fell. Matt thought of just ditching her, but because she had worked so hard to stay up with him, he decided to help her. She seemed surprised to have him offer his hand to help her up. He helped her get her skis back on, brushed her off with his mittens, and they started off again, this time side by side.

They were in a wonderland of whiteness. It had snowed the night before and they were the first ones on the trail, so with each step they were the very first to discover the crisp newness. He wasn't cold at all. He took off one of his sweatshirts and wrapped it around his waist. She did the same with hers. They even took off their mittens. The work of skiing kept them warm. Occasionally they would see tracks in the snow where a deer had crossed the trail. He always stopped and pointed them out to her.

At the summit they stopped to rest. They could see their parents far below, proceeding slowly up the trail toward them. Matt pulled two granola bars from a pocket and gave one to Susanne. She took it and they started eating.

"It's really nice up here," she said.

"Yeah, it's okay."

She turned to study his face. "Matt, why are you so set against our parents getting married?"

"I can't stand to see my dad forgetting all about my mom."

"He isn't. Not really."

"Yes he is. He and I used to talk about her all the time. Now he never talks about her. It's like we're all supposed to forget she ever existed. Well, I can't do that." He paused. "Do you ever think about your dad?"

"Sure I do. I wish he'd tried to make things work in his marriage instead of abandoning us. I wish he'd been stronger when temptation came."

"None of this is the way it was supposed to be."

"I guess it's like my mom says, sometimes you just have to make the best of a bad situation."

A long time passed before he said, "Do you want to hear about my mom?"

"Sure."

"When I went out for cross-country she was there for every race. One time I came in seventy-eighth out of ninety-two runners. She told everybody I ran faster than fourteen other runners. She was like that, always positive. And she did so many things for me. Things that nobody knows about. Like if I got to school and forgot my homework, all I had to do was phone and she'd bring it to me in school. I guess I just took it all for granted. The night of the accident, the reason why she went out at all was because we needed some milk for breakfast, because I always had cereal for breakfast—and she got out on the highway—and this man, he'd been drinking, he crossed over into her lane . . . She died because she wanted me to have milk for my cereal . . . So, in a way, her dying was my fault."

"Matt, you can't think like that. You can't take the blame. It wasn't your fault. Just like my parents' divorce wasn't my fault."

"Sometimes at night I dream about that night. In my dream I tell Mom not to go to the store, that I don't want cereal anymore, that I'll never eat cereal again if she'll just stay in the house and not go away in the car. And sometimes in my dream, she stays there with me and doesn't go to the store, and then I'm so happy because I know she's going to live, but then I wake up and remember what really happened, and then it's worse than before. All she wanted was for me to be happy . . . "

"She still wants that. Why, I bet she's looking down on us now, just hoping we'll work it out so the four of us can be a real family."

"You think so?"

"Absolutely."

"You think she knows about Jean, and that it's all right with her?"

"Yeah, I think she wants your dad to get married again."

"Why would she want that?"

"Well, your mom loves your dad, right?"

"Sure."

"Okay, then. If she loves him, then she wants him to be happy. And she knows he'll be happier with my mom than he'd ever be alone."

Matt nodded his head. "Maybe you're right. Thanks."

"Sure thing." She paused. "And just between us, Matt, if you ask me, you could really use a sister."

"What do I need a sister for?"

"Sisters can help a guy out. Like if sometime you're thinking about dating a girl, I could, you know, check her out and make sure she's okay for you." She paused. "Matt, do you think sometimes I could borrow some of your clothes? Like that sweatshirt or that yellow sweater you were wearing the first time I saw you?"

"Why would you want to wear a guy's sweatshirt?"

"Oh, just for fun."

"I don't know. I'd have to think about it. Besides, what do I get out of it?"

"You'll benefit plenty from me. Like, I can tell you what to do to make girls at school fall for you."

Matt's eyebrows raised. "Yeah? What?"

"Not now. I'll tell you when you're ready for it."

"I'm ready now. C'mon, tell me."

"When you turn sixteen, I'll tell you. Or maybe later. I'll know when's the right time to tell you."

"Does it have anything to do with clothes?"

"Maybe it does, maybe it doesn't."

"If I knew what it was and did it, how crazy would girls get for me?"

"You wouldn't believe it. They'd phone you every night. They'd hang around your locker just to catch a glimpse of you. They'd write you little notes. At dances they'd follow you around just hoping you'd ask them to dance. It'd be great."

"Tell me now."

"No, not now."

"Why not?"

"Because it's too powerful. I mean, you've got to use what I'm going to tell you sparingly. Besides, you're not supposed to date until you're sixteen anyway. If I told you now, you'd never make it until then. Girls'd be phoning you all the time, begging you to go with them."

"C'mon, Susanne, tell me."

"Just one word, and then I'm not saying another thing until you turn sixteen. You ready?"

"Yes."

"The word is *empathy*."

"Empathy? I don't even know what it means."

"When you turn sixteen, I'll explain it all to you, but not now."

"Tell me now."

"No, don't push it. I'm holding back from saying more for your own good."

He noticed she had a smirk on her face and realized she might be conning him. He picked up some snow and tossed it at her. She skied off down the hill a little way and then stopped and called back, "That does it. I'll never tell you now."

He threw a snowball at her but missed. They raced downhill. He was surprised he couldn't catch her. After a few minutes they met his father and Jean.

"Hey, where are you two going in such a hurry?" Jean called out as they sped past.

They both stopped. "Down to the car," Susanne said.

"Matt, how far is it to the top?" Jean asked.

"About five more minutes uphill."

"Well, after all this, I'm not going to just turn around now. I want to make it to the top. But I need someone to go with me so if I fall down I'll be able to get back up again. Matt, will you go with me?"

"Okay."

And so Matt's father and Susanne headed downhill while Matt started up the trail again with Jean. They had to stop once so Jean could get her breath. "If I'd have known it was going to be like this with your dad's family activities, I'd have gone into training before I met him."

"Part of it is altitude," Matt said. "Even I can notice it's harder breathing up here."

Jean laughed. "You're sweet to say that, even if it isn't true."

Finally they made it to the top. "We did it!" Jean shouted. "Oh, look at that! It's beautiful here, isn't it? I've never felt so good about winter before. I'm not even cold. It was worth it just to have this view. Thanks for coming up here with me. I'd have never made it without you. You'd better stick close to me going down. I fall a lot."

"All right."

At first going down was easy; all they had to do was keep their skis parallel and push with their ski poles. But eventually they came to the bottom of a ravine and had to climb back out in order to continue the long downhill descent.

Matt skied beside her. "What will you do with my Mom's dresses when you move in? They're in the closet. We didn't want to just give them away."

Jean glanced over at Matt. "What do you think we should do with them?"

"I don't know. We didn't want to give them to charity, because they wouldn't really appreciate them, but we didn't want to throw 'em away either. So we just left them in the closet. But I suppose you'll want to move your things in there after you and Dad get married."

"Well, yes. It would be handier to have my things in the closet. But hey, I don't have much. Maybe we could leave them in there for a while longer."

"Okay. Maybe there's even some of them you could wear."

"Maybe so, Matt, we'll see."

"You know, after it first happened, when Dad was gone, I'd go in and just sit on the bed and stare at those dresses and try to imagine Mom was just gone shopping and would be back in a minute." He paused. "I never told anyone about that before. It sounds weird, doesn't it?"

"Not at all. I know it's been hard on you."

"Will I have to call you Mom?"

"No, call me Jean."

"Do you ever bake cinnamon rolls?"

"Well, I have a couple of times. Why?"

"If you ever do, I don't like raisins in 'em. Mom knew that about me."

"All right. What else? I want to know anything that'll help us all to get along."

Matt smiled. "Get a long what?"

Jean looked confused.

"It's a joke," he said. "When we had family prayer, Dad

always used to say, 'Help us to get along.' And after the prayer Mom'd say, 'Get a long what?' "

"Oh, sure, I get it. We'll have to pull that on Susanne someday, okay? By the way, what do you think of my daughter?"

"She's okay." He paused. "She said that sometime she'd tell me the secret of what'll make a girl go crazy for a guy."

Jean laughed. "That girl . . . don't you put too much stock in what she says or she'll have you wearing your shoes on the wrong feet just because she says it's the thing to do."

"Where is she going to stay when you guys move in?"

"Your father says there's another bedroom downstairs. I suppose she'll go down there."

"It's kind of cold down there in the winter. If you want, I could switch with her, and she could have my room."

"Oh, Matt, you don't need to do that."

"I don't mind."

"Well, that's really good of you to offer."

"Can I ask you a question?"

"Sure."

"Was it hard to have your husband leave you for another woman?"

"Yes, very, not only for me, but for Susanne too. She lost a lot of respect for her dad. It may be years before they'll be able to talk again. I think it's going to be nice to have your dad and you around, so she'll know there's still some decent men left in the world."

"She's all right, I guess." He paused. "Except for one thing."

"What's that?"

"She said she might want to borrow some of my clothes."

Jean laughed. "If you let her do it once, you'll never be able to find anything. She'll have everything you own scattered on the floor of her room. So lay down the law and tell her she can't wear anything of yours. I'm serious, Matt. I have sweaters she borrowed that I haven't seen for months."

On the way home, between bites of lunch, Matt leaned forward and asked, "Dad, when are you two going to get married?"

"When do you think it should be?" he asked.

"Anytime you want. I'm ready."

"Great," his dad said. "Let's do it, then."

"Dad, if you want a little advice, I can tell you what you need to have a successful marriage with Jean."

"What's that?"

"Empathy, Dad, empathy." And then he started laughing.

Susanne poked him in the ribs. "That's it, Matt. I'm never telling you another thing about girls. You'll have to learn it all by yourself."

When they got back into town, Jean invited them in for some hot chocolate. Just before they left, Matt's father suggested they have their first family prayer. He asked Susanne to give it.

" . . . And help us to get along . . . "

Susanne couldn't figure out why Matt and her mother were giggling during the prayer.

Three weeks later they became a family.

Saturday Morning Fever

For a few brief seconds after he woke up, Steve Caldwell felt fine. He'd been dreaming that he was hairy beyond belief, a recurring dream for him since his mission and the loss of some of his hair.

Then the memory of the date he'd had the night before thudded into his consciousness like a lead ball. He sat up on the edge of his bed and gloomily looked out at the snow swirling past his window.

"Big snowstorm today," his roommate announced. "The interstate's already closed."

"Do you know how many girls at BYU have told me that they like me only as a friend?" Steve asked. But his roommate left the room, leaving the question hanging in midair.

Steve sat and brooded. An hour later, however, a sudden great idea flashed into his mind, causing him to hurriedly get dressed.

"Where are you going in this weather?" his roommate asked as Steve bundled up in his parka.

"If they can send a man to the moon, the least they can do is give me hair!" With that, he was out the door. His car wouldn't start, but undaunted, he trudged through knee-high drifts.

The first thing he noticed about the usually busy BYU

First published in the *New Era*, January 1982

health center was that there were no cars in the parking lot. In fact, there was no parking lot, only a field of snow. He climbed over a drift near the front door and walked in.

"I'm sorry," the girl at the reception desk told him, "but the doctors aren't in yet because of the storm. You'll have to wait."

"For how long?"

"I don't know. I'm only the receptionist."

"Do any of the doctors do hair transplants?"

"I don't know. I'm just the receptionist."

"I see."

The waiting room was empty except for a girl reading a magazine while breathing noisily through her mouth. He sat down opposite her and alternated between reading a magazine about tooth decay and watching her struggle for breath.

She looked up from her magazine suddenly and caught him staring at her.

"You've got a bad cold," he said.

She burst out crying.

"Nothing to cry about. Everybody gets 'em."

"It's not that!" she sobbed, fumbling for a tissue in her purse. "I was going with a guy, and last night he broke up with me. I cried all night."

"Really? The same thing happened to me last night."

She stared at him. "You cried all night?"

"No. My girl broke up with me, too."

"It's rotten, isn't it? Had you been going together very long?"

"Two weeks," Steve admitted.

"That's not very long."

"It was to her. Last night she told me she could never get serious with a guy who had less hair than her grandfather."

"How cruel."

"It was, wasn't it. What's your name?"

"Jodi Benson."

"I'm Steve Caldwell." He stood up, walked over to her, put out his hand, had second thoughts, and withdrew it. "Okay if I don't shake your hand? You can't be too careful these days."

She looked at him strangely.

"Germwise, I mean," he clarified.

He returned to his chair. "Well, there are always other fish in the sea, hey?"

"Not for me," she cried. "I need tall fish."

He lowered his eyes to the magazine and tried to figure out what she meant.

"I'm taller than your average coed," she explained.

"You don't look so tall to me."

"That's because I'm sitting down."

"Oh, sure. Well, even so, you're no King Kong."

Her lips began to curl downward, and he knew he'd said the wrong thing. Hoping to smooth things over, he added, "I mean from here you don't look that abnormal to me."

She started to cry again. He felt terrible.

"I'm not that tall," she finally said, "but guys don't date a girl unless they're at least two inches taller."

"I've never heard that."

"Have you ever dated anybody taller than you?"

"Are you kidding? I've got enough problems."

She began crying again, and he read the same paragraph about gum diseases for the seventh time. Finally unable to stand her crying, he put down his magazine. "Look, I'm sorry. I didn't mean it the way it came out. I'm sure you're a very nice person."

She blew her nose and looked up at him. "Do you really think so?"

"Sure. And you shouldn't worry. There are plenty of tall guys on campus. I mean, just look at the basketball team."

"There are forty-seven guys in school who are at least two inches taller than me. Twenty-six of them are already married. Nine are waiting to go on missions. Eight of them are either engaged or going steady with someone else. I broke up with one last night."

He added the numbers up in his head. "That still leaves three."

"One is my cousin."

"Two."

"One is forty-two years old."

"One."

"He eats only yogurt and sesame seeds and he always carries an orange in his left hand."

"Zero. I see what you mean. You're really in a pickle."

She cried while he read. A little later, he tried again. "I never knew there was so much tooth decay."

"Where I grew up, we had fluoride naturally in the water."

"I bet you don't have very many cavities, do you?"

She started to answer but stopped to touch her cheekbone. "My sinuses are killing me. It feels like my whole head's been pumped with Jello."

"I'll see what's keeping the doctors."

On his way to the reception desk, he stopped at a window and surveyed the raging blizzard. It was impossible to see twenty feet beyond the building.

"Nurse?" he asked the girl at the desk, who was listening to her small portable radio.

"I'm not a nurse. I'm just a receptionist."

"Right. Where are the doctors?"

"I don't know. The storm may have blocked the streets."

"Say, have you got anything for that girl? She's got a sinus problem."

"This isn't a drugstore, you know. I'm not a pharmacist."

"Miss Williams—is that your name?" he said, reading the name tag on her uniform. "Don't doctors get little samples of medicine?"

He walked to a cabinet and opened it. "Do you have a first name?"

"Of course I do."

He looked at all the packets of medicine.

"You're not trained to look in the cabinet," she said.

"Miss Williams, do you have any idea what that poor girl is going through in there? Don't you have any empathy?"

"If we have any, it'll be in the cabinet."

He finally found a sinus pill. He read the directions out loud: " 'Drowsiness may occur. Use caution in driving or operating machinery.' " He took a glass of water and the pill back to Jodi. She took it and thanked him.

"Why are you here?" she asked.

"I came to get a hair transplant."

"Do they do that now?"

"Look," he answered, feeling himself tense up, "they sent a man to the moon. They ought to be able to grow hair on my head."

"It's not that bad, really. What are you, twenty-eight?"

Steve bit his lip. "I'm twenty-two."

"Sorry," she said quickly.

"It's not the hair that bothers me. It's what people say. They're so cruel."

"I know about cruel," she agreed. "I was five ten in the eighth grade."

"If you're tall, you should play basketball."

"I do."

"I mean for BYU."

"I do."

"Oh. You really are an athlete. I always used to dream about being an athlete. Tell me, do guys ever wait outside the gym and ask you for your autograph?"

"No."

"That was the only reason I wanted to be an athlete — to sign autographs for girls."

Jodi yawned. "Wow, that pill is really making me sleepy."

A minute later, she was asleep in her chair.

Steve finally gave up on his magazine and turned on the TV in the waiting room, but after four commercials, the screen went blank, and he turned it off.

A little later, Miss Williams came into the waiting room. "May I have your attention?" she asked formally, as if there were a hundred people in the room. "Dr. Rawlins has asked that I close the health center and send all of you home."

"Okay."

"But just after I talked with him, I heard on the radio that they advise everybody to stay where they are."

"Do we go or stay?" he asked.

"I don't know," Miss Williams confessed. "What do you think we should do?"

He looked out again at the raging blizzard and said, "We'd better stay."

"Okay, we stay." Suddenly she noticed Jodi with her head tilted back against the back of the chair, breathing through her open mouth. "Is anything wrong with her?"

"No, she's just tired. Did you know that where she came from they had natural fluoride in the water? I bet she doesn't have many fillings in her teeth."

"Really?" Miss Williams asked.

"I've been reading about tooth decay. I wonder if she'd mind if we looked into her mouth," he said.

They both leaned over and peered into Jodi's open mouth. "Isn't that amazing?" he whispered.

"It's breathtaking," Miss Williams agreed.

"I've never seen teeth with absolutely no fillings," he continued. "I wish I had my camera."

"Really."

"She has a nice face, too, don't you think?"

"You like her, don't you?"

"I don't know. Maybe. I guess we both need someone right now."

"We don't get many romances here."

"Oh, it'd never work out. She's taller than me, and I don't have all my hair. People'd always be making fun of us."

"Do you really care about people who do that?"

"I suppose you're right," he said, looking at Jodi's upper molars. "Oh, look! I see a filling way in the back. You have to get down and tilt your head over like this."

Miss Williams also looked. "Where?"

"Way back, where my finger's pointing."

Just then Jodi woke up, saw them peering into her mouth and screamed. "What are you doing?" she demanded.

"We were looking at your teeth," Steve confessed.

"Why?"

"The TV quit working," he said.

"You scared me to death. I thought at first you were vampires."

Miss Williams returned to the reception desk. Steve sat down and picked up his magazine.

"I'm sorry, Jodi. I had no right. The least I could have done was ask your permission. You can look at my teeth if you'd like."

"No thanks."

"You have amazing teeth. You can truly be proud."

"I brush regularly and watch my snacks."

He looked up from his magazine. "I bet you'll teach that to your children, too, won't you?"

"Oh, yes."

"You'll be a wonderful mother. If you have boys, you can teach them basketball."

"Girls, too."

"Oh, sure, it wouldn't matter, would it?"

"And you could show them how to be interested and

concerned about other people . . . " Suddenly she stopped and blushed. "I didn't mean to imply that we'd get married."

"It's all right."

"Don't misunderstand me. I think you're a nice guy, but it was dumb of me to imply that we'd be married in the temple and have a wonderful family."

"No, really, it's fine." He put down his magazine, walked over and sat down beside her. "Jodi, I've never said this before to any girl, but I think you're nice."

"Thanks. That's good to hear, especially after last night."

"You know," he said, holding her hand, "you remind me of a greyhound."

"I do?" she asked with raised eyebrows.

"Oh, not the bus," he said quickly. "I mean the dog . . . that is . . . I mean . . . you look like you probably run gracefully."

"People say that on a fast break heading for the basket, I remind them of a gazelle."

"One thing's for sure. Next home game you have, I'm going."

She looked down at his hand touching hers. "Is that a very good idea?" she asked quietly.

He looked at her strangely.

"Germwise, I mean," she added.

"I can take it."

They sat in silence together for several seconds before she whispered softly, "Steve, could you let go of my hand? I have to blow my nose."

While she did that, he stood up and walked to the window. Moving aside the drapes, he saw a seven-foot snowdrift.

"Jodi, you've got to see this drift."

"Oh, yes," she said, remaining in her chair.

"No, come here and see it."

"I'm afraid," she confessed.

"Snow can't hurt you."

"I'm afraid of standing up."

He turned to face her and asked gently, "You are?"

"When I stand up, you'll see how tall I am, and I'm afraid that'll change our friendship."

"But we can't go through life together with you in that chair."

"All right," she sighed, "But turn around while I stand up and walk to you."

He turned around.

"I'm walking toward you now, but don't turn around until I say. Steve, I don't think of you as a person who's shorter than me."

He could tell that she was just in back of him.

"All right, you can turn around now."

He turned around, looked at her, and gasped, "Good grief!"

She ran from the room. A second later, he ran after her. He heard a door slam, but by the time he reached the hallway, he couldn't tell which room she had entered.

"Where is she?" he asked Miss Williams.

"Second door to the right."

He ran to the door and tried to open it, but it was locked.

"Jodi!" he yelled. "Listen to me! I'm sorry!"

From inside the room, he could hear her crying.

Miss Williams appeared beside him. "I'm sure the medical staff would frown on this kind of activity going on in the medical center."

"Jodi, it doesn't matter! Jodi! Come out so we can talk!"

"No," a muffled voice answered.

"If you don't come out, I'm going to do something drastic!"

Just then the electrical power throughout the building went out. Jodi opened the door. "How'd you do that?"

"It was the storm. The power just went out."

"Oh, no," Miss Williams moaned. "What are we going to do now? We'll freeze to death."

"We'll survive. Don't worry. First thing, get some doctor's smocks we can put on to keep us warm."

A few minutes later, each wearing a doctor's white smock, they sat down behind the reception desk. Steve took charge. "Now we're going to tell stories and play games and have a nice LDS get-together until the storm lets up. It'll be just like a long ward activity."

"How long?" Jodi asked.

"I don't know."

"Can we play Simon Says?" Miss Williams asked eagerly.

"Later. First I want to tell you about my mission."

"Then can we play Simon Says?"

Suddenly they heard yelling outside. The door opened and a student staggered in, his clothes caked with snow. He wearily stumbled to the reception desk, saw Steve, and cried out, "Doctor, you've got to help me!"

"Well, actually . . . " Steve began.

"I've been so depressed lately. This morning I even thought about committing suicide. You've got to help me, or I don't know what I'll do!"

Steve glanced down at the name tag reading Dr. Rawlins on the smock he was wearing, and then up at the student. "What would happen if you couldn't see a doctor today?"

"Don't you understand what I'm saying?"

"I see," Steve said. "All right, I'll see you. What's your name?"

"Frank Henderson."

"Before we start an examination, we need you to fill out a form. Miss Williams, get a form."

"What form?"

"Any form!" Steve whispered. "Have him fill it out in a room down the hall."

As Miss Williams escorted Frank down the hall, Steve called out, "Frank, take all the time you want filling out the form."

After depositing Frank in a room down the hall, Miss Williams ran back to the reception desk, nearly hysterical. "What are we going to do?"

"Don't ask me! I'm not a doctor!" Steve said.

"We could phone a doctor and ask him what to do," Jodi offered.

Miss Williams dialed the number and summarized the situation concisely: "Dr. Rawlins, there's a student here who says he's terribly depressed! What do we do?" A long pause followed. "I see." Another long pause. "Yes, doctor." A few seconds later. "Oh, rats!"

"Oh, rats?" Steve asked.

"The phone just went dead."

"Well, what did he say before the phone went dead?" Steve asked.

"He said for us not to let him leave the building. Dr. Rawlins will try and find some way to get here."

Just then, Frank returned with the completed form, which he handed to Steve. "Now what? I've had plenty of counseling before, but none of it's done any good. What do you people do?"

Steve felt all three of them staring at him. He cleared his throat. "Of course it varies with the individual case. There are a number of different treatments possible."

"Believe me, I've had 'em all. What will you do for my case?"

Steve picked up the form and pretended to be examining it. Finally, he cleared his throat and announced as officially as he could, "We could play Simon Says."

"Oh, good!" Miss Williams said.

"Wait a minute!" Frank said suspiciously. "I've never heard of that therapy before."

"It's new," Jodi said. "You could say we are the pioneers in Simon Therapy."

"Okay, everybody line up against the wall," Steve said. "I'll be Simon."

"Really, you should be Dr. Simon," Frank suggested as they lined up.

"Simon will do. By the way, Frank, why were you so depressed this morning?"

"Because I'm a failure."

"I see. Well, let's begin. Jodi, Simon says, take two regular steps forward."

Jodi took two steps forward.

"Frank, Simon says, take two regular steps forward."

Frank wiped his brow, put his fingers over his mouth, and stared at the floor. "No, I can't do it. You're trying to trick me."

"No, I'm not. Go ahead, you can do it."

Frank took two steps forward. "Look, I did it!"

"Good. Okay, Miss Williams, Simon says, take two tiny steps forward."

She did so.

"Frank, Simon says, take two giant steps forward."

"How big is a giant step?" Frank asked apprehensively.

"It'll vary with the individual."

Frank nervously ran his fingers through his hair. "No, I don't trust giant steps. Go on to someone else."

"All right then, Frank, just take two regular steps forward."

Frank took the two steps.

"Oh no you don't!" Miss Williams yelled. "He walked, and you didn't say Simon says!"

"Miss Williams," Steve warned.

"Those are the rules! He has to go back and start all over again."

"I knew you were out to get me!" Frank yelled.

"Nobody's out to get you!" Steve yelled back.

Frank slumped to the floor in utter defeat. "I've failed again! Everybody is ahead of me, in every class, in every job, in everything!"

"For crying out loud! Frank, get up! Don't you know that you've got to have failures in order to succeed? There's nothing wrong with having to start all over again. It's a part of life. You only fail if you quit. And doing yourself in would be the ultimate in being a quitter."

Frank stared at the floor for several seconds and then said quietly, "But I'll never be a nuclear physicist."

"So what?" Steve said. "Neither will I."

"But it's the only thing I've ever wanted to do all my life, ever since I started to watch science fiction movies about the brilliant scientist who saves the galaxy from destruction."

"What's the problem?" Jodi asked.

"Calculus. I can't pass first-semester calculus."

"Calculus? What's that?" Jodi asked.

"If I knew what it was, I could probably pass it."

"Well, you know what they say," Miss Williams said, "if at first you don't succeed, try, try, again."

"I have. This is my fourth time to take it. I flunked it the first three times."

"Oh."

"It isn't fair," Frank complained. "Life isn't fair. I want to be nuclear physicist, but I can't do math."

"I know what you mean," Steve agreed. "I want to have lots of hair, but look at me now."

"And I want to be average in height, and look at me," Jodi added.

"I want to be a nurse and I'm only a receptionist," Miss Williams said.

They all went into the waiting room and sat down and brooded. "So, what do we do?" Frank asked. "Give up?"

"The things that are important to you aren't important to me," Jodi said. "I mean, I don't care if Steve has a whole head of hair or not. If he hadn't mentioned it, I wouldn't have paid any attention to it. Life is more than hair."

"That's right," Steve said. "I don't care if Jodi is tall or not. Life is more than being average in height."

"And I certainly don't care if Frank isn't a . . . what?" Miss Williams added.

"Nuclear physicist," Frank said.

"That's it!" Steve said. "We've all been worried about what we can't be. What we ought to concentrate on is what we can be. I'm a nice guy, and I like working with people."

"And I'm a good athlete," Jodi said.

"And a good receptionist is very important to a medical staff," Miss Williams said.

"And I can be a science fiction writer and write about the brilliant scientists who save the galaxy from destruction!" Frank added.

The electrical power went back on, and Frank and Miss Williams hurried to see if the phones were working yet. Steve and Jodi sat across from each other.

"I should apologize," Jodi began. "I've been acting as if I were shipwrecked and you were the only life raft in the sea."

"And I've treated you badly," he admitted.

"You know, I feel much better now. I found out that I was the one who was making height a barrier to my own happiness."

"And I was doing the same thing, being so self-conscious about my lack of hair that I drove girls away."

"I can hardly wait to use my new insight to meet other guys," Jodi said grimly.

"Me too," he added sadly.

Then he walked over and sat down beside her. "Jodi, don't walk out of my life. We should be more than two life rafts passing in the night. Will you go out with me, at least until someone taller comes along?"

"I'd like that," she said, suddenly happy. "Besides I really look up to you."

Ten minutes later, three snowmobiles pulled up in front of the building. Dr. Rawlins jumped out first and ran to the door. "I just hope we got here in time!" he yelled to the two policemen following him. They rushed in to save the day but instead found four students in doctor's smocks dancing to music from Miss Williams's portable radio.

Sometimes They Call Me Brother

Every year it's the same before the football game between Ridgewood and Central, the two high schools in town. Each school does everything it can to fire up for the big game. On Thursday night there's a pep rally in the parking lot where the symbol of the opposing team is burned in effigy.

Another tradition, one which is not appreciated by school officials, also takes place during the week. A group of students go to the opposing high school and leave their mark. One year a group from Central painted Ridgewood's sidewalk with a large C for Central Cougars. The next year Central High was broken into and an old car painted with Ridgewood colors was driven onto the gym floor at night, and then the wheels removed. It was not until noon that authorities finally removed the car.

Unfortunately, in some people's minds it's more than just a game. Since most students attending Central are of Mexican heritage, and most at Ridgewood are white, sometimes the cross-town rivalry is just an excuse to promote racial prejudice.

For as long as anyone can remember, it has always been the same.

Jason Miller played the trombone in Ridgewood High's marching band. On Thursday night he attended the pep rally because the band had to play for it. Afterwards he went home and watched TV for a while, but then decided he'd better start studying for an algebra test. It was then he realized he'd left his algebra book in the band room at school. He would have to go back to school and get it before the janitors locked up for the night. He drove to Ridgewood High, parked, got out, and walked to the door.

"Hey, where do you think you're going?" a voice called out.

Jason stopped. Two large guys stepped out from the shadows. "What are you doing here?" one asked.

"I'm in the band," Jason said. "I left my algebra book in the rehearsal room and I've got a test tomorrow."

"I've never seen you before. How do I know you aren't from Central and you come here to make trouble."

"I've got my activity card here."

"Let me see it." Jason showed him his card. "All right, go ahead, but you'd better be telling the truth, because if you're not, and we catch you messing around . . ."

"I'm telling the truth."

"All right, you can go."

Just then they heard shouting from the other side of the building. "There's people inside with cans of paint!" someone yelled.

The two self-appointed guards ran inside the building.

Jason walked to the band room on the third floor. He could hear people yelling back and forth and the sound of running. "There they go!" someone shouted.

Because Jason was a section leader, he had a key to the rehearsal room. He went inside and began searching for his algebra book. Suddenly a girl ran into the room. She was dark-eyed, with black hair and olive skin. She was breathing hard from running. "Hide me, okay?" she asked.

She's from Central, he thought to himself.

"You can't stay here. I'm going home now and I've got to lock up."

"Just let me stay here until they've gone."

One of the student guards barged in, saw the girl, and yelled out into the hall, "I got one!" He turned to the girl. "Where'd your friends go, huh?"

"They all got away."

"Think you're pretty smart, don't you?"

Two guys rushed in the room.

Jason looked at the clock. If he didn't start studying soon, he'd really blow the test tomorrow. "Can you all go someplace else? I've got to close up now, and I can't let you stay in here because there's thousands of dollars of musical instruments and . . . "

"Hey, cool it. We'll be out of here in a minute. First we have to decide what to do with our prisoner."

"I think we should make her clean up the mess where she and her friends painted on the wall."

"I don't want to sit around and watch some chickie clean walls."

"Let me go, okay?" the girl said. "C'mon, a joke's a joke."

"I think we should keep her our prisoner and make her wish she'd never come here tonight," the one in charge said.

The smile on the girl's face vanished.

"Yeah, let's teach her a lesson she won't ever forget," another said.

Jason could see the girl was getting scared.

"Let's take her for a ride in my car."

The girl's lip started to quiver. "Please let me go."

"No way. Hey, I just thought of something. I've got some handcuffs in my car."

"Good, go get 'em."

The girl made a break for it, but they caught her and held her. "Let me go!" she pleaded.

"You're not going anywhere. Go get the handcuffs like I said."

When Jason began speaking, he realized how thin his voice was compared to the others. "I think you should let her go."

"Hey, geek, who asked your opinion? Look, just walk away from here and go home and forget you ever saw any of this."

He'd never stood up to anyone before and these guys were big and mean. But he had to say something. "I can't let you hurt her."

"Why not?"

"I just can't, that's all."

"Oh, I see, you love Mexicans, is that it?"

"No, but—"

"But what?"

"You're scaring her."

"You think we care? Look, whatever happens to her is her own fault. She was the one who broke in. You can't let these people get away with anything. She's got to be punished."

"What are you going to do with her?"

"I don't know. But it'll be so bad she'll never come back here again, that's for sure."

The girl had the look of a trapped animal. She kept trying to free herself, but it was no use. Jason spoke to the girl. "I won't let them hurt you."

The ring leader shoved him backwards. "What are you going to do to stop us?"

Jason didn't know. They were all so much bigger than he was.

The handcuffs arrived. Two of them held her while the other put the handcuffs on her. Jason saw the phone on the band director's desk. He went to it and picked it up and started to dial.

"What are you doing?"

"I'm calling the police."

One of them grabbed the phone from his hand and ripped it out of the wall. "Let's take both of them with us. Handcuff Twinkle Toes to the girl too."

A few minutes later Jason and the girl sat in the back seat of an old, beat-up car, a guard on each side of them. Jason could hear her terrified, shallow breathing. He leaned over. "Don't worry. They're not going to hurt you."

She reached out and grabbed his hand and held on.

Fifteen minutes later the car left the highway and started down a nearly abandoned road that led to a place called Crescent Ridge where people went target shooting. No more than a dozen vehicles used the road in a year's time.

"Let's all think of things we can do to our prisoner when we get to the end of this road," the driver said. Each took his turn, describing various forms of cruelty. The girl held on tightly to Jason's hand.

Suddenly the car stopped. "Let Twinkle Toes out here. We'll take the girl on with us alone."

"No," the girl pleaded.

"He's still handcuffed to the girl," the guy next to Jason said.

"Well, undo it, stupid."

"I can't see nothin'. How about turning on the dome light?"

"It doesn't work. Get in front of the headlights."

Jason and the girl were pushed out in front of the car. One of them took the key to the handcuff from his pocket and waved it in Jason's face. "You're lucky we're letting you go—you're luckier than she's gonna be."

With his free hand Jason hit the hand holding the key. The key flipped into the air and landed somewhere off the road. In the sand at night it would be nearly impossible to find.

"He just threw away the key!"

The driver got out of the car. "What's wrong with you,

anyway?" He shoved Jason backwards. Because he and the girl were bound together by the handcuffs, they both fell to the ground.

"Now what do we do?"

"Hey, they're such great friends. Let's just leave 'em here. Let 'em try walking back in the dark. It'll serve 'em right. They deserve each other. I'm tired of this anyway."

They got in the car and drove away.

The girl was quiet for a minute; then she started sobbing. Jason kept saying it was all right now. After a while she calmed down.

"Maybe we'd better start walking toward the highway," he said.

"Okay."

At first their progress was slow because it was hard to see, but eventually their eyes adjusted to the darkness.

"Why did you help me?"

"I don't know. I just did."

"You must have had a reason."

"It's the way I was raised."

"How do you mean?"

"I was taught that a guy should protect the girl he's with."

"You weren't exactly with me."

"No, not exactly."

"Who taught you that about girls?"

"The church I go to teaches that. I'm a priest."

She snickered. "You're no priest."

"In my church I am."

"What church is that?"

"The Mormon church."

"You a priest? In my church a priest looks like a priest. I'm a Catholic."

"Well, I bet that's a nice church too."

"I go every Sunday," she said.

"No kidding? Me too."

"I don't want you to think my church says it's okay to do vandalism."

"I don't."

"Do you have any tissues?" she asked. "I have to blow my nose."

"No, sorry."

She wiped her nose with her sleeve. "I don't usually do that," she said.

"Yeah, sure."

"I just don't want you going around saying we do that."

"I won't."

"People do things like that, though. Sometimes when I go in a store, salespeople stare at me like I came in to shoplift. Maybe one time they caught one of us shoplifting, and now they think we all do that. I think that's wrong. That's what makes people prejudiced."

He paused. "When I was nine years old, I got a bike for my birthday. Two days later it was stolen. The police found it over on San Marco Street, all smashed up and broken. After that I figured every Mexican kid I saw was the one who'd stolen my bike."

"Hey, it wasn't me, okay?" she teased.

They started laughing.

"What's it like to be . . . like you are?" he asked.

"It's great on our side of town. It's only when we cross over we get hassled."

"Sometimes I wish my skin was dark like yours."

"Why?"

"I can't ever get a tan. I'm either white or sunburned. It's really embarrassing when I go swimming. One time a girl told me my stomach looked like the underbelly of a dead fish."

She started laughing.

"What's so funny?"

"You are. You're very funny, but in a nice way. What's your name?"

"Jason Miller."

"That's a good name. It kind of fits you."

"What's yours?"

"Rita Sanchez."

"Rita's a nice name, too."

They walked for a time without talking, and then she said, "This is so strange."

"What is?"

"Me taking a walk with a guy named Jason Miller."

"I know what you mean."

"If we saw each other on the street, I'd never talk to you," she said.

"I wouldn't talk to you either. But it has nothing to do with prejudice. I don't talk to many girls anyway."

"Why not?"

"I don't know. Bashful, I guess."

"You shouldn't be bashful. You've got more to offer than most guys."

"Me? What have I got to offer?"

"You're a nice guy. There's not many nice guys around anymore."

"Maybe I could come see you once a week and you could pump me up by saying things like that to me."

She paused. "Sure. What side of town would we meet on?"

"I don't know. Maybe we could talk on the phone."

She nodded her head. "Sure. Except I should tell you I'm going with someone. He doesn't like whites and he doesn't like me talking with other guys. His name is John."

"Is John big?"

"Yes."

"I knew it. Big John. And mean too, right?"

"To others, but not to me."

"Big and mean, huh?" Jason paused. "Maybe if you just send me a letter once in a while."

She laughed. "You're so funny."

"Nobody else laughs at what I say."

She stopped walking. "I can't believe you were willing to get yourself beat up just to try and protect me. I wish my parents could meet you. I know they'd like to thank you too. Maybe we could have you over for dinner sometime." She paused. "Would you come if we asked you?"

"Sure. I love Mexican food." He paused. "I've got a question. Whenever I go out to eat, I always get Mexican food because it's different from what my mom fixes most of the time. So I was wondering, well, like if you go out to eat, do you ever order mashed potatoes, canned peas, and roast beef?"

She looked at him strangely and then started laughing again.

"I didn't think it was that funny," he said, pleased that she appreciated him.

"Why do our two schools hate each other so much?" she asked.

He thought about it for a minute. "I guess because we don't know each other."

"It's not right to hate an entire school, is it?"

"No. Especially if there's people like you at Central."

"And people like you at Ridgewood." She paused. "Jason, you know what? I'm really sorry I broke in. I was brought up better than that."

"I know. I can tell you're really a good person."

They started walking again.

"We ought to try and change the way things are between our schools," she said.

"How?"

"I don't know. Like if I could talk to the kids in my school and you could talk to the ones in your school."

"Sure, why not? I could ask to speak to the band sometime." He paused. "It might make a difference."

There was a prolonged silence.

"Do you really think it would make any difference?" she asked.

He sighed. "No, not really. I guess everybody's got to find it out for themselves. Like we did tonight."

They had made it to the highway. Across the street was a truck stop. They would have to cross the highway and walk inside and ask to use their phone. He knew people would stare and make jokes at their expense. After they phoned, her parents would come and her father would use a hacksaw to free them and then they would be separated and it would never be the same for them again.

"Looks like we made it," he said quietly.

"Thanks for being such a good person." She leaned her head on his shoulder for a minute and then looked at him and smiled. "You'd make a good Catholic. You could even become a priest."

He smiled. "Hey, you forget, I already am a priest."

"Father Jason," she teased.

"They don't call me that."

"What do they call you?"

"Mostly just Jason." He paused. "Well, sometimes they call me brother."

"I will call you brother then too," she said.

They walked across the highway to the glaring lights of the truck stop.

The Quiet War

Troy knocked on the door of room 803. Mrs. Palmerton, his high school teacher, opened the door, but only a crack because of the chain lock. "Yes?" she asked, her voice weak.

"I got the Alka-Seltzer you wanted."

She opened the door wide enough to take the package. Troy could see beads of sweat on her forehead.

"Are you still throwing up?" he asked.

"Twice since you left for the medicine. Maybe it's the flu—or food poisoning. Except we both ate the same thing on the plane, didn't we?"

"Yeah, whatever it was."

"Troy," she said, her voice momentarily resuming the authority of a teacher, "be sure to practice your presentation tonight. Remember you give it tomorrow morning at eleven o'clock. If I get to bed now and rest, I'll be okay by then. Now here's twenty dollars for supper. You can eat downstairs in the hotel restaurant. But don't go outside by yourself tonight, will you. New York isn't a place you can just walk around in. There are pickpockets and gangs and who knows what else waiting out there to prey on tourists like us. So just stay in your room tonight. But tomorrow, after your presentation, we'll take one of those nice bus tours where you don't actually have to get out . . ."

First published in the *New Era,* October 1981

She would have continued but she got sick again and had to leave him.

His room was next to hers. All their expenses were paid for by the school board back home in Idaho as a reward for his winning the state competition. He entered his room and chained it the way Mrs. Palmerton had told him. Then he walked to the window and looked out. Across the street was a building with cubicle offices stacked in endless rows and columns. There were people in the offices. He wondered what they did all day.

Half a block away stood a huge billboard of a girl wearing designer jeans. She was winking at him. Farther away, down a side street, he could see a flashing neon sign outlining a workman's form. It flashed consecutively oranges, reds, and pinks.

On the street, January winds swooped through the concrete canyons, giving momentary life to the cardboard and plastic litter. Taxis and buses and black limousines driven by men in dark suits honked and intimidated their way home.

It was 4:30 New York time, but only 2:30 on his watch, which was still set to Mountain Standard Time.

He took one last disapproving glance, then turned from the window.

At least I can always watch TV, he thought. On top of the TV he discovered a small metallic black box. In front there was a white button and below that, three black buttons marked "A", "B", and "C."

A poster on the box told about full-length uncut movies available to hotel guests. All you had to do was to push the white button then one of the lower buttons to make a selection. The cost was only five dollars and was automatically added to the bill. A booklet described which movies were being shown that day. Two of them, the ones designated by "A" and "B", he had seen, but not the third one. Movie "C" was X-rated.

The booklet said that by turning to channel 3 he could see a preview of the three movies available that night. He decided it wouldn't hurt to see the preview.

When the preview was over, he realized he was in trouble. He wanted to watch movie "C." He watched the preview one more time, then became ashamed for even watching that, and then turned the TV off and began to pace the floor.

The white button and then the "C" button, he thought. *That's all there is to it. It's all done with a computer. Nobody would even know.* Mrs. *Palmerton will know when she pays the bill,* he thought. *No she won't. The bill will just say I saw one of the three. I can tell her I saw the "A" movie. There's nothing wrong with the "A" movie. She doesn't need to know. Besides, it's her fault I'm trapped in this room tonight anyway.*

In his hometown there was a theater that only showed X-rated movies. People had tried to close it down but had never succeeded.

One time in priesthood meeting the priests' adviser asked if they had ever thought about going to any of the movies at that theater.

"Troy, how about you?"

"I guess I've thought about it, but I'd never go."

"Why not?"

"With my luck you'd drive by just as I was going into it," he said, only half joking.

"Is that the only reason you don't go?"

"No. I don't go because I know it's not good to have that stuff in your mind."

He stood before the black box, touching its smooth surface. *Nobody would know,* he thought. *It's all done with a computer. Nobody knows what you watch.*

He turned the TV on to see what was on the network channels. News and reruns and a cooking show with a lady plucking a goose. *Nothing good on,* he thought, turning it off again.

He returned to the window. The girl in jeans was still winking at him.

But she winks at everybody, he thought. *Millions of people a day.* He went back to the TV and looked up the movie schedule. The next showing of movie "C" was at 5:30. *It's just a movie,* he thought. *It's not going to kill me to see a movie.* He looked outside and thought how dirty everything looked.

Finally he took some hotel stationery from the desk and sat down and drew a long line down the middle of the page. On the left he put a heading, "Why I should," and on the right another heading, "Why I shouldn't."

Quickly he wrote down the reasons why he should watch movie "C": (1) Because I want to. (2) I don't have anything else to do. (3) Nobody will know. (4) How do I know it's bad unless I see for myself?

Then he listed the reasons why he shouldn't watch it.

The first reason he listed was: Karen. Karen was a girl in his ward. They had dated for the last few months.

"Do you know when I like you most?" she asked a few weeks ago.

"When I wear my after-shave and my sweater and get to use my dad's car," he answered.

"No, not then," she smiled. "It's in sacrament meeting when I watch you break the bread and bless the sacrament. You look so, well, clean."

He grinned at her. "After all the money I've sunk for after-shave you tell me that."

"It must be neat to hold the priesthood, to realize that the Savior was the first one to give that prayer and that in a way you're standing in for him."

"I've never thought about it like that before," he said quietly.

Another time he had driven her home from church. They sat in the car while she told him about her lesson that day. The bishop's wife had come to talk to the Laurels.

"She said one thing that really impressed me," Karen said. 'You never know but that the guy you're dating may some day turn out to be your bishop. It happened to me, didn't it? You treat him like a future bishop.' So that's what I'm going to do, Troy."

He wasn't sure if he really wanted that or not, but it turned out okay. She still let him kiss her, but now only on the steps to her house, not in a parked car.

The second reason he listed was: The bishop would find out. *He'd find out because I'd end up telling him,* he thought.

It was only a month since he had had an interview with the bishop.

"Are you morally clean?"

"I think so."

The bishop didn't leave it at that. "What does it mean to you to be morally clean?"

"Well, you know," he stammered, "keeping your body clean, and things like that."

"Okay—what kinds of things?"

Bit by bit Troy told what he understood. With each new addition to the definition, the bishop had asked, "And are you free from that problem?"

At that time the bishop was satisfied. But if he pushed the "C" button, the next interview would be different, because he knew he wouldn't lie to the bishop. *The bishop would be disappointed in me,* he thought, staring at the "C" button.

The third reason on the list was: Dad.

It was just over a year since his father had ordained him a priest. He still remembered part of the ordination. "Always remember the priesthood isn't like a suit coat you can take off when you enter a room. The priesthood goes wherever you go. Don't take it into places or situations where it doesn't belong."

The fourth reason was: It won't tell the truth about love.

Three years ago his mother had brought home from the hospital her sixth baby, a girl named Becky. He had held her that first day she was home and touched her tiny fingers and toes. She was beautiful to him.

His mother nursed Becky, and Troy sensed that the experience was good for the baby, to have the time and closeness with her mother.

Troy knew his mother and father loved each other very much, even more than they loved any of the children in the family. They kissed and hugged in front of the children and held hands sometimes in church. *That's love,* he thought, *not like movie "C."*

The fifth reason was: God would know.

Even though I am alone in the room, he would know what I do. I can't hide anything from him.

The last reason: I would know.

He finished the list and stood up. It was 6:00. He had missed the 5:30 showing of movie "C."

I've won, he thought. *I am strong. Nothing can weaken me.*

He decided to go down to the lobby and look around. There was a store in the lobby, and he decided to buy some gum.

At eye level, there were magazines with pictures on the covers like none he'd ever seen in the small grocery store in his hometown.

I could buy one of those, he thought. *No, I'd be too embarrassed to buy one. The lady at the cash register would wonder what kind of person I am to buy something like that.*

It doesn't matter. I'll never see her again.

I've got to get out of this rotten place, he thought, leaving suddenly.

He walked around the lobby and watched people and tried to imagine what they were doing in the hotel. Some had French or German accents.

A few minutes later he returned to his room. He turned on the TV to see what was on the regular channel. More news and a mayor telling New Yorkers to fix the drips in their faucets.

I'm strong, he thought. *I could watch the preview again and still not push the "C" button. Nothing can weaken me.*

He watched the preview again, and the same battle erupted all over again. The next showing was at 7:30—just forty-five minutes away.

Then after that, he thought, *there's one at 9:30, then 11:30. I'm going to give in sometime—it might as well be now.* He glanced at his list on the desk, read it again, then crumpled it up and threw it away.

Looking outside, he saw the flashing lights blinking on and off outlining a woman's form in harsh reds, oranges, and pinks.

Then he watched the preview again. Finally he turned it off. Except for the noise from honking taxis, the room was quiet, but inside his head a battle raged on, and he knew he was losing.

He walked to the set and glared at the buttons as if they were the enemy. *The white button and then the "C" button. That's all there is to it.* The TV was off, and he knew it didn't count, but he pushed the white button and then the "C" button.

Now just turn it on and do that, he thought. *It's so easy. Nobody will ever know. It's done by a computer, and computers don't care what you do.*

"No!" he said loudly.

He turned and sank to his knees by the bed.

"Father in heaven, I need help, and I need it now."

He pleaded with the Lord for help and, when it was over, he decided he had to leave the room until 7:30 had passed. He put on his jacket and went downstairs.

I should eat sometime, he thought, walking aimlessly

around the hotel lobby. *It's 5:30 in Idaho—Mom is fixing supper.*

On his third lap around the lobby he noticed a list of churches on a bulletin board. He decided to see if the Mormon church was listed. It was.

If I skip supper, I can go there and see what it's like. In his pocket he felt the twenty-dollar bill Mrs. Palmerton had given him for supper. He remembered she had advised him not to go out because of the bad things that lurked outside, but they didn't seem as threatening as what lurked in his own room.

He walked outside. A man in a red uniform asked, "You want a taxi?" He nodded his head.

The man put a whistle to his lips and blew hard. A taxi, one of a long line, pulled up. The man in the uniform opened the door and Troy got in.

"Two Lincoln Square," he said, faking confidence.

They drove very fast through the streets. He enjoyed looking at the passing buildings. In a few minutes they were there. The ride only cost three dollars.

He stepped out and looked around and wondered where the church was.

There he saw two girls, talking quickly in Spanish. They entered a door of a building on the corner. *They look like Mormons,* he thought, following them inside. The first thing he saw was a display case telling about the gold plates. A lady sat at a desk and smiled at him.

"May I help you?" she asked.

"I'm a Mormon from Idaho."

"How nice. My husband and I are serving a mission here, but we're from Pocatello."

When her husband came down, she let him take over while she showed Troy the visitors' center. There was a lifelike scene of the Prophet Joseph Smith in the grove.

When they finished the tour, he asked about the two girls he had seen.

"They belong to the Spanish-speaking ward that meets here also. They have activity night tonight. If you'd like to look in, we can get on the elevator and I'll show you where to go."

When he stepped out of the elevator, it was just like any Mormon meetinghouse. They were having a dance in the cultural hall. He walked inside and sat down to watch.

A lady was teaching the group how to dance the rhumba. Their only problem was a lack of guys. A girl walked up to him, and in a machine-gun-like stream of Spanish, asked him something.

"What?" he grinned.

She started to laugh.

"I'm from Idaho," he said.

She didn't seem to understand, so he tried another word she might know. He pointed to himself. "Cowboy."

"Cowboy?" she asked in awe.

"Cowboy."

She called one of the guys over and pointed to Troy and said, "Cowboy."

"Cowboy?" the guy smiled. He knelt down, challenging Troy to an arm wrestling contest.

Before long they all gathered around and watched. The two were evenly matched, but finally Troy's arm began to ache, and he lost. His opponent laughed and began slapping him on the back.

A minute later, the girl grabbed his arm and took him out on the dance floor. He didn't understand the words of the dance instructor, but he could watch and learn. Before long he had it down.

Then it was time for refreshments. He and the girl ate and giggled.

The bishop came over and introduced himself. He spoke English, too. The girl's name was Maria, and the guy he'd arm wrestled was her brother. They'd come to the states a few months ago. Maria and her brother had been members of the Church only three weeks.

Maria began talking very seriously, and although he couldn't understand the words, he knew she was bearing her testimony.

They danced for half an hour more, then they had a closing prayer. Before they left the cultural hall, Maria gave him a huge crepe paper flower used as a decoration for the refreshment table.

They went down to the first floor. When the bishop came, Troy asked him how he could get a taxi.

"Easy," the bishop smiled. He walked a little way into the street and stuck his arm straight up. A few seconds later, a taxi pulled up and stopped.

Troy got in the taxi, waved at them, and said with a cheerful confidence, "Take me to the New York Hilton."

A few minutes later he entered his room. It was 10:00. The phone rang. "Troy, is that you?" Mrs. Palmeton said. "I've been calling for the past hour. I was so worried. Where have you been?"

"I took a taxi down by Lincoln Center and went to a dance. I learned to do the rhumba and the bossa nova."

She gasped. "You went outside?"

"I took a taxi."

"But who were you dancing with?"

"Friends."

"You have friends in this town?"

He smiled and thought about the Church. "I have friends in every town."

She gave him a parting list of instructions, then hung up.

He placed the crepe paper flower on the TV. It was so big it covered up the black box.

A few minutes later, his teeth brushed, and pajamas on, he took one last look outside. *Nice town,* he thought to himself.

Companions

The day after returning from his mission, Ben Jansen remembered a promise made to his last companion. Rummaging through his wallet, he found the scribbled number and dialed.

"Hello, is this Sue Hopkins?" he asked after she answered.

"This is Susan Hopkins."

"I'm Ben Jansen."

After a long pause, she asked, "Should that be important to me?"

"Until yesterday I was Elder Wallace's companion."

"You were David's companion?" She squealed with delight. "How is he?"

"Just fine. He asked me to call and say hello, except he said your name was Sue."

"Since he's been gone, I've decided I like Susan better. How long were you with him?"

"Six months four days and eight and a half hours."

"So you must have gotten really close to him."

"Oh yes, he was a wonderful companion. So neat and clean. We painted the kitchen four times while I was with him—couldn't get the right shade at first."

"Did he tell you about me?" she asked.

"You like catsup on your scrambled egg sandwiches."

First published in the *New Era*, June 1982

"He told you that?" she asked.

"We were discussing odd eating habits. He couldn't understand the way I ate."

"Oh," she said politely. "Why? Do you eat funny?"

"I had a few stomach problems while I was with him and ate a lot of yogurt. I was afraid of getting an ulcer."

After a long pause, she asked, "Didn't you two get along as companions?"

"Oh, did I give you that impression?" Ben chuckled. "We got along just fine. Oh sure, there were problems at first, but with the help of our mission president, we worked them out."

"What problems?" she timidly asked.

"Nothing, really. I grew to love the guy."

She gave a sigh of relief. "That makes two of us. After he's released, we plan on getting married."

"You can be proud of him. He's a wonderful missionary."

"I know."

"One thing you should know—he snores like crazy."

"Very bad?" she asked uneasily.

"Unbelievable. It shook the entire apartment, but I adjusted to it."

"You did?" she asked, her voice betraying her concern. "How?"

"I slept on the porch. Of course, in the winter it was cold, but they say it's healthy."

After another long pause, she asked, "What else did he say about me?"

"He talked about how you two were a team, and how you'd bake bread and raise a garden and sew his clothes and raise chickens and milk cows and work as an auto mechanic and a secretary while he finished college."

"Oh," she said, clearing her throat. "Of all the companions you had, how would you rate David?"

"For cleanliness," he said emphatically, "I'd rate him the very highest."

"But as far as being able to get along with others, how would you rate him?"

Seconds slipped by as he desperately tried to find a diplomatic answer.

"Hello?" she said. "Are you still there?"

"Just thinking."

"Was it that bad living with him?" she asked.

"No, really. It was fine."

"Would you have wanted to spend more time with him?"

"Gee," he stammered, "I learned so much from him. I don't think I could have stood it to learn another thing."

"Please, will you tell me the problems you had with him?" she pleaded.

Suddenly his fight for diplomacy was lost. "Have you ever painted a stupid kitchen four times in six months?" he exploded. "Other elders played basketball on diversion days, but not us. No, we went to paint stores and compared color swatches!"

He realized his sudden outburst had stunned her, and he felt rotten. "I'm sorry. I don't know what got into me. I love him like a brother, and I wish you both every happiness. Good-bye."

"Don't hang up! I have more questions."

"I've been unfair to him. We had good times, too. It was just a little personality conflict, but I'm sure you'll get along with him just fine. One word of advice—decide on the color of your apartment before you marry him."

"Can you come over to my dorm so we can talk?" she asked.

It was an hour's drive from his home to her dorm. When she answered the door, he had a hard time recognizing her from David's description. Instead of a timid clinging vine, he was met by a confident, athletic-looking girl. They said their hellos and sat down on the couch in the dorm living room.

"You're a lot different than I pictured you," he said.

"How did you picture me?"

"Shy and dependent, always leaning on David for protection. But you don't look like a leaner to me."

Her warm smile made him feel very comfortable.

"I was only seventeen when I met David my first semester here. Being from a small farming community, I guess I was scared, and he helped me so much. He even helped me pick classes to take."

"Like what?"

"Just before he left, he had me taking typing, auto repair, and midwifery. He wanted me to learn practical skills to bring in money after we were married and he was in college."

"Auto repair?" Ben asked. "Could you look at my car? It's got a little pinging sound."

"I didn't take any more courses like that after he left," she said. "Tell me about the problems you had with David."

"You must think we were at each other's throats, but missionary work is too important to let personality conflicts slow it down. Actually we hardly argued at all. I just learned to adjust. I'm sure the experience will make me a better husband. In fact, every potential husband should have a chance to live with him for a while to learn to adjust."

"Give me an example," she asked.

He gave her an embarrassed look and said, "You'll think it's such a little thing."

"If it was important to you, I'd like to hear about it."

"Well, one time I made a special dessert, a plum pudding. It took half our diversion day, but it turned out great."

"I'd like to get your recipe," she said.

"David just wolfed it down, didn't say a word, and then left the table for me to clean up."

"And that made you feel unappreciated, right?"

"He could've said something," Ben grumbled. He noticed the worry on her face and added, "But I'm sure he'll compliment you on your cooking. You're probably a very good cook."

"I don't know how to make plum pudding," she confessed.

"Take my advice—don't bother to learn."

"What else did he say about me?"

"He kept saying he was the sunshine of your life, and how much you needed him. It sounds nice, but to tell you the truth, it's not my ideal. I want my wife to be a partner."

"Oh, I agree," she said quickly.

They found themselves looking at each other with a puzzled expression.

"Did you have someone waiting for you during your mission?" she asked.

"Yes, she's married now."

"Oh, I see."

"Have you dated much while David's been gone?" he asked as innocently as he could.

"Not up to now, but . . . "

"Yes?"

"Time changes a lot of things."

"Oh, but I wouldn't want you to date just anyone. You know how returned missionaries are on this campus. No sir, for David's sake, I'd better take you out a few times—just until he gets back, of course."

"That'd be nice," she purred.

And so they dated. Their common interests led them to go skiing and play raquetball and swim and go dancing. And that was just on their first date.

It didn't take more than a month before he realized he was in trouble. The social standing of a returned missionary who goes home and falls in love with his companion's girl is just next to that of a snake—except snakes are held in higher regard.

The night before David returned, they took a long walk.

"I guess I won't be seeing you much after tomorrow," he said.

"Maybe not."

"He's a lucky guy."

"You've been a real friend to me," she said.

"Susan, I've never told you how I feel about you. I promised myself that until David got back and you decided about him, I'd just be a friend. The last thing I wanted to do was take his girl away from him."

"I can't be transferred like the title to a car. You can't take me away from him, can you? It's a decision I make myself, but I owe him a certain loyalty, at least until tomorrow."

The plan for David's return was that his family and Susan would meet him at the airport. Unfortunately, three hours before the plane was to arrive, his family called her to say they had all come down with the flu. They asked if Ben and Susan could pick him up.

The plane was on time. As David came into the terminal from the plane, he saw them, rushed forward, and was buried in their hugs.

As they left the airport, David suggested they drop by Temple Square. They walked around for an hour and then decided to have something to eat at the coffee shop of a nearby hotel.

"Hey, Elder Jansen," David said, giving the waitress the menu after they'd ordered, "this is just like old times, isn't it—us eating together again?"

"Yes," Ben said, wondering if he should order some yogurt.

"Ben and I had some great times as companions, Sue."

"Her name is Susan," Ben said.

"He worked hard when he was with me. I made sure about that."

"I always worked hard," Ben added, anxious that Susan not think he'd been lazy on his mission.

"Yeah, but you let down once in a while," David said, grinning smugly.

"When?" Ben challenged.

"When I suggested we paint the living room."

Ben took a long drink of water before he trusted himself to speak again.

"I never complained, Elder. I even held my tongue when you said you developed an allergy to washing dishes."

"Please," Susan said, "don't argue."

"We're not arguing," Ben said. "We're discussing; that's all. While I was with David on my mission, we concentrated on working together, but there were always a couple of things I wanted to discuss, and now we can. I just want to say one thing, David. I slaved all day making you a nice plum pudding and what thanks did I get?"

"Plum pudding?" David asked. "What plum pudding?"

"Oh,yeah, and I suppose you forgot the nice lemon sauce on top of it too?"

"David," Susan suggested, "I think you should thank Ben for his pudding."

"I don't remember any pudding."

Ben realized his face was beet red. Susan placed her hand on David's shoulder and pleaded, "I'm sure it was a wonderful pudding. What harm is there in thanking him?"

"It must not have been that great if I can't remember it, right?"

Susan turned next to Ben. "Aren't you forgetting something? You haven't thanked David for all he did for you. I bet he must've cooked some yummy dishes for you."

"That's just it," Ben grumbled, "he never cooked anything. He said he was allergic to the kitchen. I cooked everything, I washed everything, and what thanks do I get?"

Susan nervously wiped her forehead and sighed, "Good grief! I feel like a marriage counselor. Look, let's just drop the subject, okay?"

At that point the soup and crackers arrived. They all were relieved to be able to concentrate on the food. Ben looked up to see David grabbing half a dozen crackers and crumbling them into his soup, leaving one cracker for Susan and himself to share. He didn't even look up as David slurped his soup.

After the meal was over, they walked around the lobby of the hotel.

"Sue, you really deserve an award for waiting for me," David said, looking at a five-hundred-dollar necklace in one of the hotel shops, then moving on.

"Her name is Susan."

"Typing up all my notes and sending cookies once a month."

"Cookies?" Ben asked. "What cookies? I never saw any cookies while I was with you."

"Oh, well . . . " David stammered.

"You held out on cookies?" Ben cried.

"Well, I . . . "

"Is that what kept coming in those packages? When did you eat 'em?"

"Well, I may have nibbled on one or two in the morning while you were in the shower."

"How could you hold out on cookies?" Ben asked.

"I didn't want you to get cavities," David said.

Ben looked forlornly at Susan and muttered quietly, "He ate cookies without me. That's the lowest thing a companion can do."

"No, it isn't," David said. "We talked about that once after a zone conference, and we decided the lowest thing an elder can do is go home and fall in love with his companion's girl."

Ben started to cough. When he could finally speak again, he looked at Susan and said, "He ate your cookies without giving me a single one."

"Look, if you want," she said, "I'll make some just for you."

"I hardly think that would be appropriate," David objected.

"Why not?" Susan asked.

"It's not right for a girl who's engaged to bake cookies for another guy."

Susan touched David's hand gently. "I think we need to talk about that some more."

David pursed his lips thoughtfully and gave in. "Okay, one batch of cookies."

"That's not what we need to talk about," Susan said.

"We'll talk about cookies later," David said. "Right now I want you to remember back two years when we were here for supper. It was the night before I entered the mission home. Remember, my neighbor, the one who used to work here, gave us a tour of one of the bridal suites because he knew we were planning on getting married after my mission. Do you remember that, Sue?"

"Her name is Susan," Ben said.

Before Susan could object, David was at the desk making arrangements for the manager to show them the bridal suite. On the way up the elevator, Ben stood close to her on one side, with David next to her on the other side.

"Planning a wedding, huh?" the manager asked.

"Sure are," David grinned.

The confused manager looked at the three of them and asked, "Which one is the groom?"

"That's funny!" David roared. "Sue, he thinks Ben'd marry you. No, I'm the groom, and Ben here is just an old missionary companion."

The manager let them into the vacant suite.

"Will you look at that?" David said, looking at the walls. "Sue, look, they've painted the room since we looked at it two years ago."

"It was painted last spring," the manager explained.

"What's the name of the color?" David asked.

"I'm not sure," the manager said.

"It could be honey butter . . . but it might be toasted coconut too," David said.

"Nobody ever notices the color," the manager said.

"Hey, Sue, what do you think if, after our honeymoon, we paint our bedroom this same color?"

"Oh, no," Ben moaned, shaking his head.

"Of course, we'd want to get it the same exact shade."

"You poor girl," Ben said, patting her on the back.

"Hey, this'd be a super time to make it official to announce our engagement," David said cheerfully.

"David," Ben said, "you've only been home from your mission for an hour. Wouldn't you like to go home and unpack before you get engaged? You need to get to know her again."

"Sue and I know each other."

"If you knew her, you wouldn't call her Sue."

"Sue, Susan, what's the difference?"

"David," Susan said gently, "you're not the sunshine of my life anymore, the way you used to be."

"I'm not? Who is?"

"Me."

"Boy, talk about conceited."

"With you I was always little Sue, the shy girl you helped sign up for auto repair and typing. I've grown up and overcome my fears. I can't go back to being Sue again."

"You're not my little Sue?"

"I'm afraid not."

"Excuse me," David blurted out, "I'll be waiting in the car. I need some time to think." Then he rushed out of the room.

"Well, that's it," Susan said, shrugging her shoulders. "Two years to the day, and now it's over."

"You waited for him. You sent him cookies. Nobody could've done any better."

"I'd like to close up the room and get back to the desk," the manager announced.

"Susan," Ben said, wiping away a tear from her cheek, "I told you I wouldn't say anything until you made up your mind, and now you have."

The manager looked at his watch. "I really have to get back."

"Could we see the view of the temple from the window?" Ben asked, trying to set the stage.

Reluctantly the manager opened the drapes.

"I love you, Susan. Let's get married in the temple and reserve the room for a month from now."

Susan sat down. "I've heard of people being fast on the rebound after breaking up, but this is ridiculous."

"Will you marry me?" Ben asked.

"What about the other one?" the confused manager asked. "The one who said he was going to marry her?"

"The reservation will be just for her and me," Ben said.

"I don't know, I don't know," Susan said, shaking her head. "Give me a little time to think."

They rejoined David down in the car and headed for home. He sat and brooded as they traveled along the interstate. Finally he said, "Sue, I have something to say. I know you waited for me, but I don't think this is going to work out. I think we should break up. Now, I know this is a shock for you, but I'm sure it's for the best."

"Okay, David," she said, "if that's what you think."

Ben interrupted. "I have a little something to say too. After you left, I asked her to marry me."

"You asked Sue to marry you?" David gasped. "In the five minutes I was waiting in the car?"

"That's right," Ben said.

There was a long pause. Finally David snapped, "You're just trying to get back at me because of the cookies, aren't you?"

"That's not it. I love her."

Nobody spoke for five minutes.

"Are you going to marry him, Sue?" David asked.

"I don't know what I'm going to do."

"Don't do it, Sue! Look, I lived with him for six months, and the most sickening sight I ever saw on my mission was watching him use dental floss. And his dirty socks—he just throws 'em on the floor and expects me to pick 'em up."

"But at least he knows me the way I am now," Susan said.

"So you might end up marrying him?"

"Yes, David, I might."

"Well, let me tell you something!" David said. "While I was waiting in the car, I had a chance to remember back. And you know what?"

"What?"

"THE PLUM PUDDING WAS AWFUL!"

They rode several miles in silence. Finally David turned to Sue and said, "It's not too early to begin thinking about the color for your kitchen."

"I made up my mind!" Susan cried out.

"All right!" Ben shouted. "I'll make the hotel reservation as soon as I get home, and we'll need to get temple recommends."

"Rats!" David complained.

"I'm going to do what I always wanted to do, and that's go to BYU in Hawaii next semester. It'll give me time to decide about marriage. Besides, I may never get another chance to go there. Ben, will you take me home first?"

They all sat in silence until they reached her dorm.

"I'll write every day," Ben said, as she entered the dorm.

"I will too," David added.

Then Ben continued south to David's house.

"You ought to have Sue look at your motor to see what that funny noise is," David suggested.

"I already asked. She says she doesn't know anything."

"Are you going to start college next semester?" David asked, breaking the silence again.

"Yeah."

"Living at home?"

"No, I decided to live in Provo. It's an off-campus apartment."

"Any vacancies in your apartment?" David asked.

"One," Ben said, biting off the word.

"One vacancy," David said. "Mind if I move in next semester?"

"I don't think it would work out," Ben said glumly.

"There are laws against discrimination," David said.

"It's not discrimination! I just don't think it would work out!"

"Why not?"

"Because I love Susan and so do you. That's why."

"Well, then we have something in common, don't we?"

"We don't have anything in common!" Ben roared.

"Well, what about the time we fasted and prayed for the Sorensons? And what about the Johnson family we taught and baptized? We have that in common, don't we?"

Ben remembered back to the spiritual times they had shared, when they had felt the influence of the Holy Ghost. That influence had united them in spite of their individual differences.

Several minutes later, Ben quietly said, "All right, you can move in."

"Thanks."

"On one condition. If you mention, even mention painting a room, you're out. Do you understand?"

"Clear as a bell," David said.

After letting David out at his home, Ben drove back to Provo. On his way, he stopped by a grocery store to pick up some yogurt. He wondered if he'd be using it on a regular basis now.

Jeremy Cargo—Live for the First Time in Utah

The only time Megan Riley listened to anything other than classical music was when she was in someone else's car. She was majoring in music at the University of Utah. She was a cellist in the Utah Symphony, and also the cultural arts reporter for the university newspaper.

On Friday at 5:00 P.M. Megan got a phone call from the editor of the campus paper. "Are you planning to go to the rock concert tonight?" he asked.

"Me?" she asked.

"Probably not, right?"

"Right."

"Look," the editor pleaded, "you gotta help me out. David's sick and can't cover the concert. Somebody's got to go to Jeremy Cargo's dressing room and get an interview before the concert. They promised us an exclusive."

"Why me?"

"I've tried everybody else. I'd do it, but my future in-laws are visiting this weekend and I can't leave them. Please, Megan."

An hour later Megan arrived at the arena. Even though the concert was still two hours away, there was a large crowd waiting to get in. As she made her way through, she overheard two girls talking. "What would you do now if he pulled up and just walked up to you?"

"I'd just die," her friend answered.

Megan approached one of the guards at the door. "I'm from the campus paper. I'm supposed to interview Jeremy Cargo before the concert."

"Don't give me that," the guard grumbled. "Get back in line like everybody else."

"I have a press pass."

He examined her pass. "All right, I'll let you in." He turned to unlock the door. The crowd surged toward it. He turned around and yelled, "Get back! It's not time yet!"

"Why does she get to go in?" someone complained.

"She's a reporter."

"I am too!" a girl yelled.

Suddenly everyone in the whole crowd was a reporter.

"Get back!" the guard shouted. He opened the door quickly, shoved Megan inside, and pulled it shut again.

Megan started down the deserted hall of the arena, heading for the dressing room in back of the stage. She wondered what she'd talk about in the interview. She had only a vague knowledge of Jeremy Cargo. She knew he was a rock star. Her fourteen-year-old sister had one of his posters on her wall, and she often played his music too loudly when Megan was trying to study.

A minute later she made it through two more guards in the hall outside the dressing room. She took a deep breath and knocked. A man with a shiny bald head and protruding stomach answered the door. "What do you want?" he snapped.

"I'm from the universtiy newspaper. I'm supposed to interview Jeremy Cargo."

"He can't talk to you now. How about if I just give you a press release?"

To Megan it looked like an easy way out. "All right."

From inside the door a voice called out, "George, who is it?"

"Just a girl from the university paper."

"How does she look?"

"Just like all the others."

"You're getting too old for this, George. Open the door and let me have a look at her."

The man opened the door all the way. Jeremy Cargo, wearing jeans but no shirt, sat in an old rocking chair strumming a guitar. He looked at her. "George, she's a beauty. Let her in. I'll talk to her."

Megan was allowed in the room.

"What's your name?" Jeremy asked.

"Megan Riley."

"Megan, this is George. He's my manager."

George nodded his head but didn't look up. He was playing solitaire. He looked like someone who'd been on the road his entire life; the late nights and fast food had taken their toll. He treated her as some unavoidable nuisance to be endured.

"Can we get you a beer or anything?" Jeremy asked.

"No, thanks. I don't drink."

"My shoulders are a little stiff. Would you massage them to help me loosen up?"

"Mr. Cargo, if you want a massage, I suggest you contact the chairman of the physical education department. He might be willing to send one of the trainers who work with the football team. The reason I'm here is to do an interview. I know you're busy, so I don't want to take up too much of your time. Can we begin now?"

He was looking at her strangely. "By any chance are you a Mormon?"

"Yes."

"George, she's a Mormon. I told you we'd meet at least one in Utah, didn't I?"

George grumbled something.

"Am I keeping you from getting dressed for your concert?" she asked.

"I am dressed for the concert."

"But you're not wearing a shirt."

Jeremy smiled. "This is what I wear on stage for the first song."

"Oh." She paused. "I see."

"Is something wrong?"

"Why would anyone go on stage without a shirt on?"

Jeremy laughed. "The girls like it. Besides, look how flat my stomach is. You wouldn't believe how hard it is to keep it that way."

"I see," Megan said. She didn't know what to say next. There was a long pause.

"You don't seem very comfortable doing this interview," Jeremy said. "What do you say we switch roles and you let me ask you a question."

"All right."

"Have you heard my latest album?"

"Actually, I'm not sure if I have or not."

"You're not sure?"

"Well, I might have. You see, my younger sister is a big fan of yours and sometimes she has her tape deck on too loud when I'm studying. I'm always complaining to her about it, but sometimes even after she turns it down, I can still hear the music through the walls, so it's possible I've heard your new album, but I'm just not sure."

"You're not a big fan of my music then, are you?"

"No, not really. The regular reporter couldn't make it so they sent me."

"Do you like music at all?"

"Yes, but I'm more interested in classical music. I play cello in the Utah Symphony."

George looked at the clock on the wall and stood up. "Jeremy, get rid of her. She's a loser."

"In a minute." Jeremy turned to her. "If you could ask me any question, what would it be?"

"Are you happy?"

He smiled. "Didn't you see the crowd outside? It's like that wherever I go. After a concert, hundreds of girls stand outside the door just waiting for a glimpse of me. If I ever get lonely, all I have to do is open my door and pick out the foxiest-looking girl and ask her in. Everyone loves Jeremy Cargo."

She smiled faintly.

"Tell me what you're thinking," he urged.

"I'd better not."

"No, go ahead. I'm really curious about you."

"I was thinking that . . . well . . . I feel sorry for you."

"What for?"

"Because you have to go around being Jeremy Cargo all the time."

The smile on his face faded away.

"I'm sorry," she said. "I guess I shouldn't have said that."

"What did you mean by it?"

"I should go now. Really. If George could give me one of your press releases, I'll just submit that to my editor—"

"Don't go. I want to know what you meant when you said you felt sorry for me."

"I was just wondering if you have any real friends." She stood up. "Look, I'm sorry the way this has turned out. I really think I'd better go now. I know you have things to do. Thanks for your time."

He stood up. "Wait. Will you be at the concert?"

"Well, no, I hadn't planned on going."

"George, give her a ticket."

George handed her a ticket.

"Will you go, as a favor to me?"

"Well, all right."

"And after the concert, I want to talk to you again," Jeremy said.

"Oh, I don't know. There'll be so many other girls wanting to see you."

"Please."

"All right."

A guard escorted her through two doors to her seat. The arena was still empty. Three guitar players and a drummer were warming up and a technician was checking out the sound system.

Fifteen minutes later she heard something that sounded like a dam breaking. She turned and saw a crowd running into the arena toward her. Within five minutes the place was packed solid with people.

The girl who had the seat next to Megan turned excitedly and said, "Can you believe this? We're actually going to see Jeremy Cargo. I love him so much, don't you?"

Megan smiled politely.

The crowd started chanting, "Jeremy, Jeremy, Jeremy . . . "

The concert began with fireworks and a white cloud rushing across the stage, and then a blackout. When the lights went on again, there he was with the other musicians. He had a red bandana tied around his forehead.

The group began with their most popular hit. The crowd went wild. Megan turned to look at the girl next to her. She was standing up, crying out at the top of her voice, her arms outstretched toward the towering presence of Jeremy Cargo.

After the ovation for the first song died down, Jeremy shouted to the audience, "I love you all!" He threw his bandana out into the crowd. The girl next to Megan caught it and started sobbing uncontrollably with joy.

Two hours later the concert was over. Megan half hoped Jeremy would forget about seeing her, but because she had agreed, she stayed in her seat as the crowd filed out. Just before she was about to leave, George came and escorted her backstage.

Outside Jeremy's room, there was a crowd of girls waiting for a glimpse of their hero. George pushed through them, Megan right behind him. He unlocked the door and they went inside. Jeremy introduced her to his backup musicians. To Megan they looked strange in their bizarre costumes and makeup. After a while they left for their own dressing room.

Jeremy looked tired but at the same time excited by what he had created on stage. "How did you like it?" he asked her.

"I was amazed how hard you work up there. You really give people their money's worth."

"Thanks. What else?"

"I was surprised."

"By what?"

"That you're such a good musician."

"You didn't expect that?"

"Not really."

Jeremy smiled. "George, how about that? I think she liked it."

George scowled. He had no use for Megan.

"I'm sorry, but what's your name again?" Jeremy asked.

"Megan."

"I'm sorry. I meet so many people. After a while names just fly past me. Megan, how about if we go have a drink?"

"I don't drink."

"Not ever?"

"No."

"I keep forgetting you're a Mormon. Well, let's go out for a glass of water, then."

"I don't think so, but thanks."

"I take it you didn't fall in love with me at the concert?" he asked with a smile.

"No."

"Everybody else did."

"I think you're right." She stood up. "I really need to be going now. Thanks for taking the time to talk to me."

"Wait. Before you go, I have a song I want to sing for you. I wrote it during intermission in your honor. I call it Megan's Song." His fingers caressed the strings of his guitar and he began singing. It was a quiet love song. Every verse had her name in it.

He finished. "And that's Megan's Song. What do you think of it?"

"It's a beautiful song."

"You should be honored. It's not every day Jeremy Cargo writes a love song for a girl."

She smiled. "Last night by any chance was that song called Mary's Song or Karen's Song or Jenny's Song?"

He laughed. "What a skeptic you are!"

"You didn't answer my question."

"Maybe, but tonight I really mean it."

There was a knock on the door. When George answered it, several girls tried to rush in, but the guard stopped them. It was an older woman who had knocked. She was from the main office. She said something to George in hushed tones.

George shut the door. "Jeremy?" he said.

"What is it?"

"The office just got a phone call. You need to phone home right away. There's been an emergency."

"What is it?"

"You'd better phone home and find out."

"Did they tell you what it was?"

"Yes."

"Well, don't keep me in suspense. What is it?"

George paused. "It's about your mother. She's had a heart attack."

"How bad is she?"

"I really think you'd better phone the hospital."

"You know how she is, don't you? Tell me."

George couldn't look Jeremy in the face. "She's dead.

She died on the way to the hospital. It happened a couple of hours ago. It's taken them this long to find us."

Jeremy's face grew pale. He played a few chords on his guitar and then looked up again. "I'll need to go home, George."

"I'll make all the arrangements." He paused. "I should go to the office and use their phone. Is it all right if I leave you here alone?"

"I'll stay with him," Megan said.

George nodded and left.

"I'm really sorry about your mother," she said.

He turned away and wiped his eyes and then started strumming his guitar softly. Several minutes passed. "She gave me this guitar," he finally said. "It was the first one I ever had. I was twelve years old at the time. It was right after my dad died. Mom got work in a factory. We had to move into a smaller apartment on the fourth floor of a dingy building. On my birthday she gave me this guitar. And it's been with me ever since. I used to tell her that someday I'd be rich and famous and buy her a house in the country. She'd just smile and say that all she wanted from life was to see me happy. And now she's gone." He sighed. "Gone forever."

"Not forever. I know where she is now."

"What do you mean?"

"She's with your father and all the other relatives who passed away before her. She's happy there. Don't worry. She's okay. She doesn't want you to worry about her."

"How do you know all this?"

"From the Bible and other scriptures. Life doesn't begin with birth and it doesn't end with death."

"Are you sure about that?"

"I'm sure."

He looked at her for a long time and then sighed. "For some strange reason I believe you." He stood up. "Do you mind if I take off my stage makeup while we talk?"

"No, go ahead."

He sat down in front of a mirror. "My mother was like you in some ways. She was a very religious woman. Went to church every week, I think mainly to pray for my soul. She worried about me all the time. She always talked about me finding a girl and getting married and settling down. I'm sure she had someone like you in mind. Someone who'd tell me to wear a shirt on stage." He smiled faintly. He told about boyhood experiences and how important his mother had been in his life.

Half an hour later George returned. "Jeremy, we're still trying to round up the flight crew. We think it'll be another hour or so."

"What about the others?"

"I don't know how to get in touch with them. They went partying up some canyon somewhere. I'll call around and see if I can find them before your plane leaves. If not, I'll come later with them on a commercial flight. Also, I need to begin making phone calls to cancel your concerts for the next few days. How long of a break will you need for this?"

"Good grief, George, how can you ask a question like that now?" Jeremy said.

"I know this is hard for you, but I need to know."

Jeremy sighed. "Let's give it a week."

"I'll make all the arrangements. Oh, I've called a limousine to take you to the airport. There's still a crowd outside waiting to see you. If they see you leaving, they'll follow you to the airport and you won't have a moment's rest."

Megan interrupted. "Don't have him go in a limousine. That's too obvious. Let me take him to the airport. Nobody'll pay any attention to us."

George looked at her with an expression bordering on respect. "Good idea."

Ten minutes later a custodian wearing Jeremy's clothes

was escorted by guards into the limousine as hundreds of eager fans pushed and shoved for one glimpse of their idol. At the same time, Megan and Jeremy walked undetected out to her car.

At the airport, she drove to a charter office, far from the regular terminal. A man let them in, then closed and locked the door. "We've just located the pilot. He was at a ski resort just out of town. He's driving down now. I'll let you two in my office to wait."

They went into the small office. Jeremy sat down behind the cluttered desk and cradled his head in his hands. Megan went out and found some cups and a pot of hot water. She made two cups of hot chocolate, then carried them back to the office. She came up behind him and rested her hand on his shoulder. "Jeremy, would you care for some hot chocolate?" she asked.

He took the cup. "Thanks."

"Sure."

"You're the kind of woman my mother wished I'd settle down with. Is there someone in your life right now?"

"Yes. He's on a mission telling people about our church."

"Where did you meet him?"

"We've known each other since we were little. He lives across the street."

"Sounds very proper."

"It is."

"I've never met anyone like you. My mom would be happy to know you." He couldn't finish. Tears streamed down his face. "I need a favor."

"What is it?"

"Tell me again about my mother, where she is now."

"She's fine. Don't worry about her."

"There really is a life after death?"

"Yes."

"And I'll see her again someday?"

"Yes, you will."

"What is it about you? When you talk about these things, I feel so much better."

"It's the Holy Ghost."

"What's that?"

The man returned. "Mr. Cargo, the pilot's just arrived. We'll be ready for takeoff in just a minute. You should proceed out to the plane now."

"I'll just be a minute more," Jeremy said. The man left.

Jeremy reached out and held both of Megan's hands. "I'll never forget you." He looked into her eyes. "With all that I have, all the money, all the fame, right now more than anything I wish I knew what you know about life and death."

"You can learn."

He thought about it for a minute and then said, "I'm afraid Jeremy Cargo doesn't do that."

"Is that your real name?"

He blushed. "No. My real name is Oliver Stewart. Awful, isn't it?"

"I think it's a good name. Do you think Oliver Stewart would want to learn more about these things?"

"I don't know. He might." He paused. "If only Jeremy Cargo will let him." He looked out at the plane and then back at her. "I'd better go. Good-bye, Megan."

"Good-bye, Oliver."

He kissed her on the cheek and then turned and walked to the plane. He bounded up the ramp, turned one last time to wave at her, and hurried inside the plane.

She watched the plane take off and then drove back home.

The Gimmick

John lingered in the hall before deciding to get it over with. He was sorry he had even come. His mother had talked him into it, saying, "After all, he is the bishop, and if he wants to see you the least you can do is go."

He's going to say he hasn't seen me at church lately, John thought as he idly gazed at the bulletin board in the hall, and they'd like me to help on some project, and I'll tell him I'm too busy right now, and he'll say they really need me and then I'll leave, and it'll be over for another six months.

He knocked on the door and Bishop Warren invited him in.

Now some small talk to loosen me up, John thought.

The bishop asked about his schooling to become an auto mechanic. John answered in two words. Then the bishop asked about his mother and dad, but John curtly reminded him that the man with his mother was his stepfather, not his real father.

"You're probably wondering why I asked you here," the bishop said.

Here it comes, John thought.

"God has called you on a mission."

The silence roared through his ears.

First published in the *New Era,* April 1983

"I don't want to go on a mission," John said.

"That's between you and God. My job is to tell you that you've been called."

He didn't tell me how much they need me, John thought, stunned and off balance.

"I'm not going."

"It doesn't matter that much to me personally if you go or not," the bishop said, "but I want you to realize that God has called you on a mission."

"This is just a gimmick to get me to shape up, isn't it?" John said.

"Is it?" the bishop asked.

"Sure, that's what it is."

"Why don't you pray and ask if it's a gimmick?"

"I don't need to pray because I'm not going."

"Tell that to God then, but not to me. Before you decide though, I have some scriptures on this card I want you to read. Will you do that?"

John avoided the question and took the card. "Is that all you wanted to say?"

As he drove from the church, his mind boiled with anger at the bishop. He wants me to go on a mission so it'll look good on his report, he thought as he slammed the car into second gear, so he makes up a story about God calling me. Well, he's not fooling me.

He had his life planned, and it didn't include a mission. First he'd get a job as a mechanic, then marry Jill and settle down. That's what he wanted in life, and a mission didn't fit in. Besides, he wasn't even going to church or living the way the Church taught. Ever since his father had died and his mother remarried a nonmember, none of them had gone to church.

A few minutes later he parked his car in front of the truck stop cafe where Jill worked and went inside. As he sat down at the empty counter, she brought him a cup of coffee, and then poured herself one.

"Well?" she asked with a grin.

"Well what?"

"What did the bishop say?"

"He said God's called me on a mission."

She barely got her coffee swallowed before bursting out with laughter.

"You—on a mission? Boy, that's a laugh."

"I'm not going."

"Did you tell him you were going to marry me?" she asked.

"I don't have to tell him anything. I just said I wasn't going."

"But you are going to marry me in June—right? I mean you're not inventing this story about a mission just to get out of it, are you?"

"I said I'd marry you," he snapped. "How many times do I have to say it?"

"You're so romantic," she said sarcastically.

Another customer came in, and she left to get the order. In a few minutes she was back again.

"This coffee tastes rotten," he complained. "What'd you do, make it with dishwater?"

She took a sip. "It tastes okay."

"It's not okay—it's terrible."

"Don't drink it then. See if I care."

Another customer drifted in. While he waited for her to come back, he tried to doctor up his coffee by pouring cream and sugar in it, but no matter what he did, it still tasted like burnt rags soaked in dishwater. Finally he put so much cream in that it ended up a chalky white lukewarm disaster. He reach over and dumped it down the drain.

A few minutes later it was quitting time for Jill. As they walked to the car, he asked, "How about going with me to the Longhorn for a beer?"

"On a Tuesday? What's the occasion?"

"I just feel like it. Besides, they have that western band playing there this week."

"You never drink on weekdays, so why do you want to now? Trying to prove how bad you are so God will let you off the hook about a mission?"

"Quit talking about that. It's over and done with."

"I don't see why you're so uptight. They'd never send anyone like you on a mission."

"What about going with me to the Longhorn?"

"Count me out. If you start drinking on Tuesdays, you're going to end up an alcoholic."

"Forget it then. I'll go without you."

"Suits me fine. You're in a bad mood, and I don't want to be around you anyway."

He took her home and went to the Longhorn, a small place on the highway that served beer mainly to the just-out-of-high-school crowd. While he was there, two guys came in. For one of them it was his eighteenth birthday, and they were celebrating by drinking one beer after another as fast as they could until one got sick and the manager made them clean it up, which made the other sick.

John walked out, saying to the one huddled on his knees pushing a towel over the floor, "That's so clever the way you did that."

At home in his bedroom he took off his shirt and found the three-by-five card in the pocket with a large handwritten message, "God has called you on a mission. Pray about it." He threw the card into the wastepaper basket, turned off the light, and went to bed.

He couldn't sleep. After two hours of tossing, he sat up in bed and said out loud, "God, I'm not going. So just forget it. Amen."

On Friday night there was a party for a group of mechanics and instructors involved in the training program. They met at a place called Al's Oasis.

About eleven that night, one of the instructors, a man named Wayne, got into a fight with his wife. As it heated up, they said things to each other that shouldn't have been heard by the group. His wife got mad and called a taxi. Wayne got drunker and more obnoxious. A while later he came and asked Jill to dance, but she said no and that made him furious. John told him to get away from her. Wayne tried to hit him, but John ducked and planted his fist solidly in Wayne's stomach, causing him to double over and fall down.

Two of Wayne's friends started to make noises about getting even with John. He thought he could handle them but was worried about Jill's safety if there was a brawl. He grabbed her hand, and they ran out the back door to the car. As they drove away, John saw another car pull out after them, and he knew there might be trouble. He had done enough deer hunting in the area to know the back roads, so after a few shortcuts, he lost the car behind them, but he kept going for several miles to make sure they wouldn't find him.

Half an hour later they ran out of gas on a little-used country road. He knew they would have to walk into town. It was a beautiful clear night with the stars filling the dark sky. It had been a long time since John had looked at the stars. He didn't say much for the first few minutes of walking, until Jill finally asked what he was thinking about.

"Wayne and his wife—the way they were yelling at each other, the way he was drinking."

"What about it?"

"That's the way we'll be in a few years."

"Is it?" she asked.

"Sure—we argue now, don't we? And I drink too much. Sure, we'll be just like them—if we stay married. But maybe we won't. Maybe we'll get a divorce."

"You are getting cold feet about marrying me, aren't you?"

"I'm getting cold feet about ending up like them. There must be more to life than that."

"What do you want, you know, in life?"

"I want to be the best mechanic in town. I'm good at it, and I like it. And I want some sons to take fishing and hunting. And I want a house and a pickup truck."

"Anything else?"

"If we marry, I want it to last."

"Me too," she said. "If we're married, I want you to be faithful to me. I don't want my life to be like a soap opera."

They walked a ways in silence, both of them feeling awkward at being so serious.

"John," she asked, "suppose we have sons. Will you let them go to Primary?"

"Why not? It can't hurt 'em—at least while they're small."

"How about Sunday School?"

"If it doesn't interfere with me taking them fishing and hunting."

"You can fish on Saturdays."

"Yeah, I guess so," he said.

She waited several seconds before getting courage to ask, "What'd be wrong if we started going to church?"

"What for?"

"For our future sons and daughters, so we can learn. Mormons know how to raise good families, and that's what we want, isn't it?"

"I'm not going," he said bitterly. "If you start, the first thing you know they ask you to do something, and before you know it, your whole life is spent at church. I don't want to get into that."

"Can we go for a few times just to see if it's as bad as we think it is?"

He looked at her, shook his head, and gave in. "All right, we'll try it for a couple weeks, but that's all."

On Sunday they went to church, and even John had to admit it was okay. While they were there, he studied the missionaries sitting with one of the families they were teaching. No way, he thought to himself.

On Wednesday he asked Jill if she would go drinking with him on Saturday night.

"I don't want to go."

"Why not?"

"I thought we were going back to church," she said.

"What's going to church got to do with enjoying a beer now and then?"

"You're the one who's always saying people who go to church are hypocrites, so now you want to be one too. Is that the way it is?"

"I agreed to go to church, but that's all. I'll drink when I want, and nobody's going to tell me to stop!"

"I will, John. You'd better stop drinking."

On Saturday night he went without her. A little past midnight he got into an argument about religion with the guy next to him, who was an atheist. John tried to convince him about God.

"There's a God," John said.

"Prove it."

"Look at the flowers. You think that just happened?"

"Yeah, that's what I think."

"You're crazy, you know that. Flowers don't just happen," John said, slamming down his mug for emphasis.

"What do you know about God anyway? What's he to you?"

John stared at the empty mug, it's promise of happiness gone, leaving only an empty froth, full of air with no substance. That's when he became very depressed.

"What's wrong with you?" the guy next to him asked.

"God wants me to be a Mormon missionary."

The guy laughed so hard he nearly fell off the chair.

At three in the morning, John drove to the church

parking lot and stumbled onto the lawn in front of the chapel.

"Hey, are you there?" he yelled, looking up at the spire. "Look at me! I'm drunk! Do you see that? Isn't that disgusting? That's why I can't go on a mission—so quit bugging me about it! Look, I'd like to help you out, but you've got the wrong person. I'm not a good person. I'm rotten—rotten to the core."

He sat down on the lawn and started to cry again. Among the sobs he pleaded, "All I want you to do is tell the bishop you were wrong about a mission for me. Then just let me be me—no good, rotten John."

After that he must have crawled into the car and fallen asleep, because the next thing he remembered was the slamming of a car door next to him. He woke up and looked around. It was early morning. Standing next to him looking into the car was Bishop Warren. "You're here early this morning for church," the bishop said.

John's mouth felt as if somebody had driven a cattle truck through it all night, and his head ached. "Bishop, last night I was drinking, and I came here to get a message to God that he made a mistake about calling me on a mission. I'm not good enough to do anything in this church."

"Do you believe now that God wants you to go on a mission?"

He looked up and said quietly, "I guess I do, but it's too late. I've made too many mistakes."

"John, you've got to learn to repent now. Let's go to my office, and I'll give you a thorough interview."

He was too tired to argue. As he opened the car door, two empty beer cans rolled onto the parking lot, making a loud noise. He stepped gingerly from the car, picked up the cans, tossed them in the front seat, and stumbled after the bishop.

In the office, he sat rigidly in his chair, feeling that the room was leaning over to one side. The bishop asked him question after question, and it was embarrassing to answer them truthfully, but he wanted the bishop to know everything about himself. After the last question, the bishop was silent for a moment and then said, "John, you've disappointed the Lord."

"I know. I'm sorry."

"Before you were born, he called you to serve a mission, and you agreed. But now, unless you repent in a major way, you'll lose that opportunity. We don't send young men on missions unless they're clean. The time to start repenting is now. Let me write down the things you need to work on. If you can turn your life around, you can still serve a mission, but it'll take a while to demonstrate your obedience."

"How long?" he asked.

"Maybe a year."

"That's a long time, bishop."

"A year's a year, whether you repent or not. And if you don't repent, where will you be after a year?"

The bishop's list filled two pages. "I'll see you next week at this same time, and we'll see how you're doing. Priesthood meeting starts in an hour, so you better get home and change."

He hurried home and got ready, making it back just in time.

After Sunday School, he talked to Jill.

"I was surprised to see you here this morning,"she said.

"I'm going on a mission."

"Sure you are," she laughed.

"No, I mean it."

She looked at him as if for the first time. "Why?"

"God wants me to go."

She looked at him for a long time before saying, "I think I'm seeing a part of you I never knew existed—the part you tried to hide from everyone." She pursed her lips, closed her eyes for a second, and then tried to smile. "Well, so much for a June wedding—right?"

"It's just two years, and when we get married, it'll be in the temple."

"I can't believe it," she said. "You and me—regular church people. Who'd ever have thought it?"

"What will you do while I'm gone?" he asked.

It took courage for her to even say it. "You know what? Nobody in my family ever went to college. What if I went to Ricks College, maybe just for a year, you know, just to say I've gone? I think I'd like to do that."

"Jill, have you talked to the bishop?"

"No, why?"

"You ought to, and when you do, ask him for the thorough interview. He writes down a list of things to work on, and you go back in a week to report how you've done."

So for the next few months, they both repented.

Six months later on a Sunday he watched a guy in faded Levi's and western shirt burst from the bishop's office laughing as he headed toward the door. John asked him what was so funny and was told that the bishop had said that God had called him on a mission.

"Isn't that stupid?" the guy howled. "I don't even go to church."

So it was a gimmick after all, John angrily thought as he stormed into the bishop's office.

"How many others have you told God called them on a mission?" he snapped.

"All young men between the ages of eighteen and twenty-five."

"I believed you when you told me! I didn't know it was just hype to drum up more missionaries!"

"Let's talk about it, John," the bishop said in an even tone.

"I'm tired of talking to you!" John said, whirling toward the door.

"Where are you going?"

"To get drunk!" he yelled, heading outside with the bishop right behind him.

"You can't go back to the way you were."

"Why can't I?"

"Because now you have a testimony. Don't you?"

He stopped just before reaching his car and thought about the past six months. The bishop was right. He had a testimony that the Church was true. He couldn't go back to the way he had been.

Inside the office, the bishop pulled a worn copy of the *New Era* and read parts of a talk by President Kimball: " 'Should every young man . . . fill a mission?' . . . The answer the Lord has given [is] 'Yes, every worthy young man should fill a mission.' The Lord expects it of him. And if he is not now worthy to fill a mission, then he should start at once to qualify himself." The bishop put down the magazine.

"But I thought you meant God wanted me personally to serve a mission."

"John, I've fasted and prayed about what I told you. God does want you to serve a mission. If you doubt it, fast and pray about it too."

He did pray and fast, and that helped him feel more assured the bishop was right, but the complete answer didn't come until three months later.

He had continued to drop by the cafe near Jill's quitting time, where he had his nightly cup of hot chocolate. One night she said, "Why don't you come with Cindy and me next Saturday? We're going to get a patriarchal blessing."

"What's that?"

"I'm not sure exactly. Cindy's mom says it's personal revelation to help a person live his life. Will you take us? We have to go out of town to where the patriarch lives, and we were hoping you'd drive us. You could get a blessing too, but first you'll have to get an interview from the bishop."

"That's no problem," he smiled. "It seems like the past year has been one continuous interview."

When he went for his interview, he brought the worn pages of repentance goals the bishop had given him on his first thorough interview. One by one, day by day over the months since then, he had checked each item.

After the interview, the bishop gave him a recommend for his patriarchal blessing and said, "John, you're clean now."

On Saturday the three of them drove to the stake center, where they met the patriarch. He talked with them for a few minutes before giving each of them a blessing.

As the patriarch laid his hands on John's head and began, it was like a cleansing shower of light and joy washing away the bad opinions he'd had about himself. As a child he had believed himself to be a bad boy, a mischievous boy, an average boy, a low achiever, a troublemaker, a bad example. He found that if you believe that about yourself, your life matches what you believe. Even at first when he tried to repent, underneath it seemed artificial, as if he were only putting on an act of goodness but deep down was still rotten and would be forever. But now as the patriarch gave him a blessing, he felt strongly that God was his Father in heaven and that as a son in the premortal existence he had once been greatly loved and trusted.

He knew he was crying and that tears were rolling in small rivers down his face, and he knew Jill and Cindy knew it too, but he didn't care because for the first time in his life, he knew his true relationship to God.

The patriarch told him that Father in heaven had called him to serve a mission, which was what the bishop had said, except this time, John knew it was true.

After the blessing, he sat in the chair, wiped his eyes, and, a little embarrassed, asked Jill for a tissue.

That's how John came to go on a mission, and why Jill saved some money and quit the cafe and went to Ricks. Sometimes she'd be listening to a lecture when she would suddenly realize where she was and she'd think, Look at me! I'm in college and I never thought I'd be, and I'm smart enough to understand what the professor is saying, and I bet there's a hundred other things I can do that once seemed impossible. I'm going to stay active and live the commandments and be married in the temple. Nobody around here, no bishop or other priesthood leader, has ever said my past mistakes were too great or that it's too late for me to repent. All that's important is that we start today and repent and live the commandments, and the Savior will take care of the rest.

John worked harder on his mission than ever before in his life. When he first started out, he thought what a great sacrifice it was to take two years to serve the Lord. But as his mission progressed he learned you can't really sacrifice to the Lord because the more you give, the more he blesses you, and when you finish, you're more indebted to him than ever before.

Sometimes on his mission he and his companion would stop at an auto repair shop. Inside John always looked for the meanest-looking mechanic there who was about his age, and he would walk up to him and say, "God sent me here to talk to you." The guy usually swore and went back to his work on a car. John would lean over the other side of the hood, peering into the engine to watch him work, and little by little he would explain the message God had for that mechanic.

During his mission it only happened once that the mechanic ended up joining the Church, but John thought it was great that one did because, as he used to say, Father in heaven needs all the mechanics he can get.

"Otherwise," he'd say with a broad grin, "in heaven, who's going to service all those chariots?"

Happiest Two Years

Elder Scott Marlow stumbled wearily out of the bus into the harsh lights of the nearly deserted bus depot. It was two in the morning, and the town was asleep except for a few stragglers who had to be up for the bus.

Although it had been a long trip, it was one that he had relished as he thought about his first assignment as a district leader over six pairs of missionaries. It was the first in a long line of goals he had set for himself on his mission.

An obviously sleepy elder approached him and shook hands. He introduced himself as Elder Derek Anderson.

"Sorry to get you out so late at night," Scott said as they threw his luggage into the trunk of the car.

"It's okay," Elder Anderson said. "But I'll never figure out why they can't run a bus schedule at decent hours."

As his companion drove him to their apartment, Scott asked him about the area. "Who are you working with? Anybody that's good?"

"Sure, the Fosters. You'll love the Fosters. They're terrific."

They met the Fosters the next night. During their meeting, Scott continually pushed for commitments from them, but they just grinned and asked if he'd like some more cake.

As they drove home that night, Scott dropped a

First published in the *New Era,* April 1984

bombshell. "If they don't accept some challenges the next time we meet with them, then we drop 'em."

"Just like that? We've been working with 'em for six months."

"Maybe they're just deadwood. We're out here to baptize."

"Give 'em some time."

"I don't have time."

The next time they met with the Fosters, Scott challenged them to prepare for baptism. They accepted the challenge. Two weeks later they were baptized.

"What's that little notebook you look at sometimes when you're studying?" his companion asked Scott one morning.

"It's a record of my goals. I've mapped out my life, step by step. So far I'm on schedule."

"Can I look at it?"

"I usually don't show it to anyone," Scott said warily, "but I guess it's okay."

His companion carefully looked through the notebook. "What's the check mark by each goal?"

"I make a check when I've accomplished the goal."

"Oh, sure. I see where you set a goal to be a district leader, and you've checked that." He continued looking. "You're going to be a zone leader?"

"I guess I shouldn't have let you look at my goals," Scott said with embarrassment. "I know we're not supposed to aspire to positions in the Church."

"That's all right," his companion replied, continuing to examine each goal. "I see you've written down a goal to baptize six months in a row. Can you really do it?"

"Sure, why not? We've already got one month. Are you willing to work for it? We can do it if we work. We can succeed."

Succeed they did. For the next five months the mission

newsletter highlighted their consecutive baptisms. The elders in Scott's district caught fire too. The number of baptisms coming out of his district made history.

The team of Marlow and Anderson seemed to complement each other. Scott was strong on helping families to set goals to pray and attend church, but his companion seemed to get along with people better. Children flocked around Elder Anderson wherever he went. Scott didn't mind, though, because they were a team.

One morning Elder Anderson came out of the bathroom with Scott's hairbrush. It was matted with hair. "Have you looked at this lately?"

"I know," Scott said dismally. "I'm losing my hair."

"Isn't there something you can do?"

"I don't know," Scott sighed. "I wish there were."

The sixth month wore on with no baptisms in sight. The tenth of the month passed, and they weren't teaching anyone who would be ready.

"Sister Johnson invited us over for dinner tomorrow night," Elder Anderson announced as they were heading home one evening after a floundering discussion.

"I hope you told her no," Scott said grimly.

"Why?"

"It'd be a waste of time. A sixty-year-old widow isn't likely to have any referrals."

"It'd be nice to have a home-cooked meal. Besides, she doesn't have many people visit her."

"Tell the home teachers. It's not our concern."

"What is our concern?" his companion asked with an edge of tension in his voice.

"To find somebody to baptize this month."

"We're already leading the mission in consecutive baptisms. What do you want, another record to add to your string?"

"Why shouldn't we succeed? We can do it if we work."

"Okay, maybe we can. But there's one thing that bothers me about you."

"What's that?" Scott asked defensively.

"You're doing all this for your own glory—so you can be zone leader."

That set Scott off. "Doctrine and Covenants, section four," he said. " 'Oh ye that embark in the service of God, see that ye serve him with all your heart, might, mind and strength.' "

"Okay, you work hard. Still I'm worried about you. The elders in the district are afraid to talk to you. They talk to me about their problems."

"What problems? They're baptizing more now than they've ever done," Scott defended.

"They feel a lot of pressure from you to produce."

"We're supposed to produce."

They walked into their apartment and got ready for bed, hardly speaking to each other.

Just before prayers, Scott gave in. "Okay, I was wrong. We'll have supper with Sister Johnson tomorrow night."

Much to their surprise, Sister Johnson had an elderly lady with her who wanted to be taught so she could be baptized. And she was, before the end of the month.

Scott received a letter from his girlfriend a week after he had written her about breaking a mission record. "We're so proud of you in the ward," she wrote. "My dad says that he wouldn't be surprised if you were made a zone leader or even an assistant to the mission president. I've been going to firesides with Mark Stevens. You remember him? He's just back from his mission."

One morning during study class, Scott picked up the mission roster and looked up the date of arrival of each of the zone leaders in the mission. One of them would be released within the month. Scott glanced through the mission newsletter to see if he could see any other strong candidates for the position besides himself. As far as he could tell, there weren't any others. He pictured his parents bragging in church that he was a zone leader. Smiling to himself, he resumed studying the scriptures.

During the week that one of the zone leaders was to go home, Scott and his companion received a phone call from the mission president asking them both to come to the mission home the next day. They both were to bring their luggage with them.

"I bet I know what that's all about!" Scott's companion said with a smile. "You're going to be the next zone leader."

Scott forced himself to be nonchalant but could not suppress a smile. "Now, now, we're not supposed to aspire to positions."

Nevertheless, Scott got his suit cleaned and carefully polished his shoes. *Look the part,* he told himself. He made sure that they left in plenty of time so they'd be there promptly.

President Snowden enthusiastically welcomed them as they entered his office. They chatted for a few minutes, and then President Snowden excused Scott while he spoke to Elder Anderson. In a few minutes, Elder Anderson left the office, and it was Scott's turn.

"Your companion has told me about your little notebook of goals. It's remarkable what you've done."

"Thank you, sir," Scott replied, properly modest.

"You must have wondered why I asked you both here."

"Yes, naturally, I did."

"Well, you know, the zone leader in Centerville is going home this week. We are looking for someone to fill his position."

"I see." Scott felt his heart pounding with excitement.

"Of course, the order of the Church is that we are called by inspiration. You believe that, don't you?"

"Yes, of course."

"Sometimes choices made by inspiration are not the obvious ones. The Lord chooses whom he will, when he will."

Scott wondered why the president didn't just come out with it and call him to be zone leader.

"When I prayed and fasted about this, I was frankly surprised the way it turned out. The Lord has seen fit to call your companion, Elder Anderson, as a zone leader."

Scott was stunned. "Oh," he said weakly, embarrassed by his suddenly reddening face.

President Snowden walked over to where Scott was sitting and put his hand on Scott's shoulder. "Remember that in the work of the Lord, it's how we serve that counts, not where we serve."

"Is that all, sir?"

"No, there is one other thing." President Snowden pulled a chair close to Scott and sat down. "Did you know that we have a city in our mission that has 80,000 people living in it, and yet we have no missionaries there? We had elders there once, but they never did much good. Part of the problem was that they believed it was the Siberia of the mission. It was a self-fulfilling prophecy."

All Scott wanted was to get out of the office.

"We're going to put a set of missionaries in that town, but we're going to put the best we've got. This time we're going to succeed."

"I see," Scott said.

"Elder, I want you to go there and see what you and the Lord can do."

"Me? But what about my being district leader?" he blurted out.

"We'll call someone to take your place. Your companion will be a new elder. He's arriving tomorrow. We'd like you and Elder Anderson to stay overnight with us before you go to your new assignments."

As Scott left the office, the president added, "If you have the time, why don't you and Elder Anderson take in the museum today. It's very good."

Scott hurried from the office. He went to the bathroom and shut and locked the door. Turning on the cold water, he soaked a washcloth and held it to his face. Feelings of anger surged through his mind.

Nobody must know how I feel, he thought to himself ten minutes later as he examined his face in the mirror before leaving the bathroom. He walked into the office area and congratulated his companion.

The museum was in the heart of the city. Urban decay had rotted away the neighborhood near the museum. They parked the car and walked along a newspaper-strewn sidewalk.

A man stood in a doorway watching them approach. He held in one hand a twisted brown paper bag containing a bottle. As they came near him, he stumbled out of the doorway toward them.

"Are you Mormons?" he asked, slurring his words.

"Yes," Scott answered.

"I thought so. Well, I've got a question for you. Do you know Jesus Christ?" The man leaned forward, thrusting his face at Scott.

"Our Church can tell you more about the Savior than any other church," Scott said.

"That's not what I want to know. Do you, yourself, know him?"

Scott felt the man's probing glare. *He's only a drunk,* he thought. *He probably has to beg for whiskey.*

"Do you know Jesus Christ?" the man again demanded.

Scott tried to move aside, but the man grabbed his coat sleeve. "Do you know Jesus Christ?"

"Let me go!" Scott ordered, jerking his sleeve and running for the museum doors. Elder Anderson followed after him.

"Tell me!" the man shrieked.

"Well, he won't follow us in here," Elder Anderson said with a smile in the museum lobby.

"Why not?" Scott asked, still shaken by the experience.

"Because it costs two dollars to get in."

They strolled through the museum corridors, following the progress of mankind from earliest times until the present. Around every corner, Scott expected to see the man charging toward him, yelling his question.

As they stood before one exhibit, Elder Anderson stood beside Scott and said quietly, "Elder, I'm sorry. I didn't even want to be a zone leader."

Scott turned slightly to acknowledge his companion. "It's all right. It's not your fault."

Several seconds passed, and then Elder Anderson asked quietly, "Whose fault is it?"

Scott looked at him, puzzled by the question.

"Is it President Snowden's fault for receiving the inspiration? Or is it the Lord's fault for giving the inspiration?"

"I'm sorry," Scott said quickly. "I didn't mean that. It just slipped out."

Scott couldn't sleep that night. An overwhelming feeling of failure crept into his throat and chest and crushed down. Dreams became nightmares. The man from the street ran through his thoughts, shouting at him the same question.

Driving to their new area the next day, Scott wondered if he had been as annoying to his first companion as this new elder was. His name was Elder Carlisle.

"Do you know that you're going bald?" Elder Carlisle asked as Scott was driving.

"Am I?"

"Sure. You comb it to get the most use out of the hair you've got left, don't you? Sort of swirl it over the bald spots, don't you?"

Why me? Scott thought to himself about his companion.

"Does your girlfriend know that you're going bald?"

"No," Scott replied glumly.

"Maybe you could wear a hat when you get home until she agrees to marry you." A chuckle.

"Do you mind?" Scott asked, annoyed at his companion.

"You're pretty sensitive about it, aren't you?"

They found an apartment that day and began work. They were the only members in the area. They spent their days tracting.

A week later Scott got a Dear John letter from his girlfriend. She was going to marry a returned missionary all right, just like they'd planned, but it wasn't going to be Scott.

"I sure hope there's a young lady back at BYU who likes a shiny scalp," his companion said with a smile. "My girlfriend will never send me a Dear John letter, though, because we're really in love."

The month passed with no baptisms. Scott's consecutive baptism record was gone. The next issue of the mission newsletter carried no mention of Scott. He did read about the success Elder Anderson was having encouraging the elders to set goals.

The next week they had a zone conference. They met in a ward meetinghouse forty miles away. President Snowden was there and interviewed each missionary. Scott was one of the first to be interviewed. President Snowden was intensely interested in the work being done in the new area.

Before Scott left after the interview, he asked if he could talk to President Snowden about something that was bothering him. "President, what do you say to someone who asks if you know Jesus Christ?"

"I guess I'd need to know the circumstance."

Scott described the incident. "Why does the question still haunt me?" he asked.

"Is it such a difficult question? Since you were a child,

you've been taking the sacrament, promising to always remember the Savior."

"I felt such an emptiness when that man kept hammering away with that one question. Why?"

"You have a notebook with goals written in it, don't you? Do you have any goals that relate to the Savior?"

"In a way, they all do."

"Let me see if I can explain. The Savior once asked the question, 'What manner of men ought ye to be?' Do you remember the Savior's answer?"

"He said that we should be like him."

"That's right. Do you have any goals to become more like the Savior?"

"No, sir."

"What if you tried to radiate love for others the way Jesus did? What if you tried to carry out your priesthood assignments the way the Savior would? Do you think it would make a difference in your life?"

"I'll never be like him."

"Wouldn't it make a difference if you tried?"

President Snowden came around the desk and put his arm on Scott's shoulder, "We have mission rules. We have commandments to obey. We have counsel from our leaders to follow. But the final requirement is to learn to follow the Master. Can you put a goal like that in your little notebook?"

They had lunch in the cultural hall after the morning meeting. As he sat down at a table, Scott's companion called over to him, "Hello, O hairless one!"

The elders within hearing range smirked.

"My companion is the only one in the mission who takes thirty minutes to wash his face. It's because it goes clear to the back of his neck."

More laughter.

Scott ate quickly and left. He found the chapel open and vacant, so he sat down and began reading the scriptures.

"Looks like you're busy as usual." Scott looked up to see the wife of his mission president. "Are you all right?" she asked with kindness.

"Do you know any way to make hair grow back?" he asked her.

"The elders can be cruel, can't they?"

He felt the pent-up frustration pouring forth as he talked to her about his problems. She listened to him attentively, and just talking about it made him feel better.

Missionaries began to file into the chapel for the meeting. Before she left to go up on the stand, she showed him a book she was reading. "Look at the author's picture on the inside cover. You can see he's bald, but do you see any fear or shame on his face?"

"No," Scott said, looking at the picture.

"He's a very positive man and, I think, handsome too. You know, Elder, you really have a nicely shaped head."

"I do?" Scott said.

"Sure you do. It'd be a shame to hide that with hair."

The next morning Scott cut his hair very short.

"What have you done?" his companion gasped as he came out of the bathroom.

"I've decided to quit hiding my good-looking head."

Before he knew it, there were only six months left of his mission. Scott felt that there still was so much to learn. For the first time in his life, the scriptures seemed to come alive for him. He cherished reading the New Testament.

He was beginning to feel a closeness to the Savior. Now, as they traveled in the car, Scott avoided the usual light conversation and instead talked enthusiastically about Jesus.

"You know," he said one morning as they drove to their tracting area, "I think the Apostles were probably always trying to keep the Savior on a schedule. I think they had so many miles to travel to get to a place to stay, and they didn't want to travel at night. But there were so many interruptions.

"One time Jesus and the Apostles were going to Jericho. There was a blind man sitting along the road, maybe begging. He heard the sound of the crowd coming. Someone told him that Jesus was coming. He began shouting for Jesus. The people told him to shut up, but he yelled even louder. I think the people traveling with the Savior were really mad because they wanted to make good time. If it had happened in modern times, they'd all have been looking at their watches. They were behind schedule.

"But the Savior stopped. He asked them to bring the man to him. They did. He asked the man what he wanted. The man said that he wanted to be able to see. Jesus looked with compassion on the man and healed him."

Scott drove in silence for several blocks. "That man was probably considered by many to be the scum of the earth. Jesus could have walked away from him—like I walked away from a man once—but he loved others so deeply."

Four weeks later they baptized a family of four. Then the brother of the wife of the first family joined. Then his wife. Then his parents. Soon they had ten members meeting in a home for a sacrament meeting.

Then it was time for another zone conference. It was a rainy April day as they got on the interstate to travel to the conference.

Scott was driving. As he rounded a curve, he saw a car pulled over to the side of the road. A young mother wrestled with a tire jack while two small children peered out the back of the station wagon at their dripping mother being soaked by the rain. Scott slowed down.

"We'll be late if we stop," his companion warned.

"I know."

"If we help, we'll get wet."

"I know," he said, pulling off the road.

"Then why are you stopping?"

"She needs some help."

"Maybe it's a trap. How do you know there's not a couple of guys hiding, ready to take our money?"

"We don't have any money," Scott smiled.

Scott stepped outside into the pouring rain. "Can I help?"

"I can't figure out how to work the jack."

"Why don't you get out of the rain? No use both of us getting wet."

He worked quickly changing the tire. As he worked, he realized that he was singing. He looked up once and saw the faces of the two children pressed against the back window of the station wagon. He winked at them and made a silly face. They both giggled.

When he was finished, he opened the back door of the station wagon and put the flat tire and jack in the back. The woman got out to thank him. "Can I pay you something?"

"No, but there is something you can do," he said, running back to his car. He picked up a copy of the Book of Mormon and ran it back to her. "Read this," he said, thrusting it into her hand. Then he turned and ran back to the car.

He had never felt so happy in his life.

"You look like a drowned rat," his companion complained as they continued down the road.

"At least my hair isn't wet," he answered, smiling.

"I suppose you know that we're going to be late for the meeting."

"I'm sorry for making you late. It couldn't be helped."

"Yes it could. You could've passed her by. Someone else would have come along."

"Will that lady ever have a better reason for reading the Book of Mormon?" Scott asked with a wide grin.

"She doesn't even live in our area. Even if she's baptized, someone else will get the credit."

Scott found himself humming.

"Why are you so happy?"

"Because I've done something that the Savior would have done."

They arrived a few minutes late. Scott's suit was soaked. Sister Snowden saw them come in and hurried over to Scott. She wouldn't let him stay in wet clothes. She talked to the custodian, who found an extra pair of coveralls for Scott to wear while his suit dried. Scott sat in the back of the chapel and listened to the conference.

President Snowden interviewed Scott while he was still in the borrowed coveralls.

"How's my goalsetter?"

"President, I've changed some of my goals. I've replaced some of them for one goal—to try to become more like the Savior."

"That's a lifelong goal," President Snowden said.

Scott agreed. "I've found out that it's true what you said. It is not where we serve; it's how we serve."

A few minutes later, President Snowden asked, "How would you feel about serving as a zone leader for the remainder of your mission?"

"I don't need it anymore. I'm content where I am, in our little branch."

"It is the will of the Lord that you labor as a zone leader."

"I'll serve wherever he wants me."

A few more baptisms, a few more meetings, a few more washings of the same eight white shirts and it was over.

He returned to the mission home for his last night before flying home. President Snowden had it arranged so that the missionaries going home and the missionaries coming into the mission field could have a testimony meeting together the night before they went their separate ways.

"I guess this has been the happiest two years of your life. Right?" one of the new elders asked him after the testimony meeting.

"What?" Scott asked, coming out of his deep thoughts.

"The happiest two years of your life—that's what all the elders say in our ward when they return."

"Happy?" Scott said. "Yes, I guess it has been happy."

"You've lost all your hair, haven't you? How are you going to find anyone to marry?"

"I'll set a goal, Elder," Scott said with a smile.

"They tell me you were a zone leader. How long did it take you to be a zone leader?"

"Why do you want to know?" Scott asked.

"Oh, nothing."

"I hope you're not planning on that as some kind of goal."

"I want to succeed on my mission," the elder said with determination.

"Look," Scott said firmly, "let me sum up two years of my life. Jesus Christ stands at the head of the Church. We are commissioned by the Savior to teach the gospel. He loves the people in this mission. You must focus your entire energy on serving Jesus by loving and serving the people."

"I know that," the new elder said confidently.

"Don't worry about artificial goals—like being a zone leader. That kind of a goal has no place in this work."

"Sure, you can say that," the new elder said. "You are a zone leader. How long did it take you?"

Scott shook his head in frustration. "Elder, you're going to learn a great deal out here."

"Oh, I don't know. I've pretty much got the discussions mastered already."

"I wasn't talking about the discussions."

"You never told me how long it took you before you became a zone leader," the new elder called after Scott as he ascended the stairs to his room.

Before he went to bed, Scott read 1 Corinthians 13 and Moroni 7.

The Goldfish Parable

The house was a raging inferno.

"It's no use," the fire chief muttered, watching the flames leap high into the air. "Pull back!" he shouted. The fire crew moved back from the searing heat.

"Help!" a girl suddenly cried out from a second-floor window.

"Oh no," the fire chief mourned.

The girl's parents, who had just returned from a movie, were quickly ushered over to the fire chief.

"Help me!" the girl shouted.

"Please save our daughter," the mother pleaded.

"I can't ask any of my men to go into that tinderbox now—it'd be suicide."

Randy stepped from the crowd. "Don't worry, I'll save your daughter."

Before anyone could stop him, he ran toward the house, paying only slight attention to the crowd's horrified gasp as he rushed into the flames.

It's a good thing I'm wearing this action jacket, he thought as he kicked the door down. Inside, the stairs were still intact, although fire was licking through several of the steps. He covered his face with the jacket and bounded up the stairs.

First published in the *New Era,* May 1986

On the second-floor landing, because the jacket was still over his face, he tripped over a tricycle in the hall, but quickly recovered and hurried to her room.

He opened the door and saw her. She was in one of his classes in high school. She had long hair and nice eyes, although for some reason he couldn't make out any details of her face. *Maybe it's the smoke,* he thought. She threw her arms around him. "I knew you'd come." she cried.

A loud crash shook the house.

"What was that?" she cried.

"The staircase caving in," he said calmly.

"How will we ever get out?"

He thought for a second then said, "I have a plan."

Running to what was left of the hall, he grabbed the tricycle and hurried back to the room. He pulled an adjustable wrench from his jacket pocket and undid the front wheel. Then he kicked out the rubber from the wheel, leaving just the metal rim.

"Anyone else in the house?"

"No—my brother is spending the night at our uncle's house."

He hurried to the window and kicked out the screen and looked out. Just as he had noticed earlier—a telephone cable ran from the street pole to within a foot of the window. He leaned out, placing the rim of the wheel over the cable, then asked her to hand him the rest of the tricycle, which he refastened upside down onto the wheel again, the forked brace holding the wheel rim in place on the cable.

It was ready. He motioned for her to climb next to him on the window ledge. Putting one arm around her waist and holding onto the handlebar with the other, he jumped out into space. They rolled gently down the telephone cable like a miniature cable car, leaving the house just before it broke apart. The crowd below roared its approval.

"Oh, Randy, you're wonderful," she sighed hugging him.

A minute later they were on the ground, surrounded by a TV news crew and several newspaper reporters. A newsman from the TV station stepped forward, microphone in hand, and asked the question on everyone's mind. "Hey, kid, whataya think you're doing?"

That's not the right question, Randy thought. He looked again at the reporter. Somehow he had changed into a store clerk.

"Look at this window!"

Randy came back to reality. He was standing in front of a men's clothing store. In front of him in the display window was a mannequin wearing a light jacket. Beside it was a poster that read, "Men of action prefer Brock Jackets."

"Just look at this!" the clerk pointed. "You've got fingerprints all over my window. What if everybody put their hands on it, hey? What then?"

"It'd get messy," Randy answered philosophically.

"Don't get smart with me! Look at this mess! You smeared ice cream on it too, didn't you?"

"That wasn't me."

"Well, somebody did."

"It wasn't me."

"Who do you think has to clean up this mess anyway? Me, that's who. So quit messing up my display window!"

Randy reached down and picked up his trumpet case and walked away. He was on his way to his music lesson.

Mr. Janowski's living room had a high ceiling and cracking linoleum floor. Stacks of music cluttered every table and chair. Even the fishbowl, complete with a small goldfish, sat precariously on top of a stack of music on the coffee table.

Randy ran through the trumpet exercises while Mr. Janowski sat back in an ancient overstuffed chair with one hand over his eyes. Randy often suspected that Mr. Janowski slept through part of each lesson, except that whenever he made a mistake, Mr. Janowski would call out, "Flat!" or "Sharp!"

The doorbell rang. Randy stopped while Mr. Janowski answered it. A father and daughter appeared in the doorway.

"I'm Arlen Reynolds. I talked to you on the phone about starting my daughter in flute lessons. We just moved into town."

"Oh yes, I remember. Come in. What was your daughter's name?"

"Michelle."

Randy whispered the name to himself. It was the most beautiful word he'd ever heard.

As they came inside, Randy stood up, hoping for an introduction, but Mr. Janowski ignored him. "If you'll come with me, I'll explain how we work the payments for the lessons."

The two adults left the room, leaving Randy and Michelle alone. He watched while she took the flute out of the case and assembled it.

A minute later she happened to drop her lesson book. He lunged to pick it up—knocking over the music stand, which hit the coffee table, causing a large stack of music to slide to the floor. The fishbowl nearly fell too, but he grabbed it at the last second. Finally he reached her book on the floor and handed it to her. "Thank you," she smiled. "Now let me help you pick up things."

On hands and knees they picked up the scattered sheet music. He was close enough to sense a delicious smell. He closed his eyes and sniffed.

When he opened them again, she was staring at him. "Probably my shampoo," she said.

He nodded his head and went back to work.

When they finished, she returned to her flute.

He followed, staying within sniffing range.

She picked up her flute and, unaware he was so close, quickly turned around.

He had to duck to avoid being hit by the end of the flute as she swung around. Falling sideways, he crashed into the coffee table, knocking over another stack of music. The fishbowl fell to the floor and shattered. The goldfish flopped helplessly on the soggy music.

He scooped it up in his hands and desperately looked around for some water.

"I'll go find a bowl in the kitchen," she said hurrying out.

Time was running out for the goldfish. Then he saw the opened bathroom door.

In the bathroom, he closed the drain to the washbasin, turned on the water, and gently dropped the fish in. Then he looked in the mirror and practiced saying the word *Michelle*.

She returned with a large soup pan. He plunged his hand into the water, splashing water on himself, but coming up without the goldfish.

"Maybe if we let a little water out, it'd be easier," she suggested.

He placed his hand on the drain mechanism, preparing to open it a little at a time.

At that moment Mr. Janowski and Michelle's father returned to see the floor covered with water-soaked music, the fishbowl broken, and Randy and Michelle looking with great interest into the washbasin.

Randy began to gently ease down the drain handle.

"WHAT ARE YOU TWO DOING?" Mr. Janowski yelled.

Randy's hand jerked downward. He looked over at the two scowling adults. When he looked back at the washbasin, the goldfish was gone.

"Young lady, I want an explanation!" her father said abruptly.

"We leave you two minutes," Mr. Janowski raged, "and look what you do!"

"It wasn't our fault!" Randy said. "If there hadn't been so many stacks of music, it would never have happened!"

Mr. Janowski picked up the broken fishbowl. "Where's my goldfish?"

"He's not dead," Randy said.

"Then where is it?"

Randy looked sadly into the empty washbasin. "On a long voyage."

"You dropped my goldfish down the drain?" Mr. Janowski asked.

"It wasn't our fault! We were trying to save its life. Besides, it's only a goldfish."

"OUT OF MY HOUSE! NEVER COME BACK! NEVER AGAIN LET YOUR SHADOW DARKEN MY DOOR! I NEVER WANT TO SEE YOU AGAIN!"

"What about next week?" Randy asked.

"YOU ARE A NUMBSKULL! GET OUT OF HERE!"

Randy shrugged his shoulders and returned to the music room to put his trumpet in its case.

"It wasn't my fault!"

"GET OUT OF HERE!"

That night at supper, sandwiched between a lively discussion by his brothers and sisters, Randy quietly announced, "I won't be taking lessons anymore from Mr. Janowski."

"Why not?" his mother asked.

"He kicked me out of his house and told me to never come back."

His father raised his eyebrows. "Oh?"

The phone rang and it was for his father. Randy quickly finished eating and went to his room to study.

An hour later he brought the hall telephone to his room, called directory assistance for Michelle's number, and phoned her.

"Hello," her father answered.

"Is Michelle there?"

"No—would you like to leave a message?"

"Okay."

"What's your name?"

"Randy."

"Randy?"

"I met her this afternoon—at her music lesson."

"Oh, you," her father said, sounding angry again.

"I'll just call back."

"Don't call tonight—it'll be too late by the time she gets back."

"Maybe tomorrow then."

"Suit yourself, but she's busy with school."

There was a long frigid pause. "Okay, 'bye."

At eight-thirty his father came in, sat down on the bed, and said, "Tell me what happened at your music lesson today."

Randy told him the story.

"It might be nice if you went back and apologized to Mr. Janowski."

"Dad, he doesn't want to see me again. Besides, it wasn't my fault—it happened because of his messy room. If I go back, he'll just get mad all over again and start yelling."

"Maybe you could buy him a new fishbowl and a goldfish."

"It wasn't my fault. You should've seen where he had the fishbowl. It's a wonder it hadn't fallen off before. I'm not apologizing for something that's not my fault."

His father looked at him for along time, then said "Okay."

Randy was puzzled. It wasn't like his father to give in so easily.

His father stood up to leave, then asked, "Hey, aren't you hungry? How about if we go for a pizza."

A few minutes later, they sat down in the restaurant and ordered a pizza.

"What happened to you today," his father began, "reminds me of something that happened on my mission. Our mission home was in New York City, across from Central Park in a very exclusive neighborhood. My companion and I were working in Long Island. On one rainy day, we had to go to the mission office for supplies. Somewhere between leaving the car and walking into the mission home, I must have stepped in some mud.

"When we got inside, nobody else was in the office. I saw the material we needed and walked over to get it. On my way back, my companion pointed out the mess I'd made with my muddy feet. I remember thinking they should have a throw rug at the entrance so that wouldn't happen.

"We were in a hurry to get back for a meeting, so we left. That night after our meeting we got a call from one of the office elders. He told us that our mission president had seen the mess and told the housekeeper to leave it. He wanted us to go back the next morning and clean up our muddy footprints.

"I tried to explain we'd been in a hurry, that it wasn't really our fault, that they should have had a throw rug, but it didn't matter. They wanted us to drive all the way into the city through all the traffic and clean up our mess."

Just then the waitress brought the pizza.

A couple of slices later, Randy asked, "What happened?"

"The next morning we drove into the city again, got a pail of water, cleaned up the mud, and went home.

"The next time we had zone conference, our mission president talked about what happened without mentioning names. He told us that in life, try as we may, we all leave muddy footprints. We don't mean to, but it happens. He said there are three kinds of people in the world—those who absolutely refuse to do anything to clean them up, those who will only clean up when they are required to, and those who see the mud and voluntarily go about cleaning up. I always remembered that. He called it the Parable of the Muddy Footprints."

"You still want me to go back and apologize, don't you?" Randy asked.

"And you still feel you shouldn't have to, don't you? Let me ask you a question—under what circumstances can you ever imagine yourself apologizing to anyone?"

"When I'm in the wrong."

"You mean when you're entirely in the wrong. When there's nobody else you can point to and say it was partly his fault too—when you're 100 percent in the wrong."

"Yes," Randy said, "then I'll apologize."

"It'll never happen."

"But why should I apologize for something that isn't my fault?"

His father looked at him for a long time, then asked, "What do you know about Mr. Janowski?"

"He teaches music lessons."

"Does he have a wife? Any children or grandchildren?"

"I've never seen anybody else at his house."

"So maybe he lives alone."

"I guess so."

"Maybe he never married, or maybe he was married and his wife died."

"Maybe—all I do is take trumpet lessons from him."

"He's not a young man, is he? Maybe he's been alone in that house for twenty years. Does he have a dog?"

"No."

"I wonder why he kept a goldfish, don't you? Did the fishbowl have a filter system on it?"

"No, it was just a bowl."

"That means he had to change the water every day. Why do you suppose he went to the trouble?"

"Dad, I don't know."

"Well, let's just imagine. Maybe he kept it for company. Maybe it gave him something to care for. Maybe he imagined the fish liked music. Maybe sometimes he talked to it, or had a name for it. On Christmas maybe he dropped a little extra fish food in the bowl. But now he's dead."

"Maybe not—if it can swim through the pipes to the lake."

"But it's gone. I wonder if he'll buy another one, don't you?"

"They don't cost much. He could afford it."

"Maybe he'll decide not to bother—then he'll be completely alone."

Randy sat and looked at his last slice. He wasn't hungry anymore. They left.

"You really think he cared about a goldfish?" Randy broke the silence on the way home.

"I don't know—but he could have. One thing though—he knows you didn't care about it very much."

Several blocks of silence passed by.

"Dad, I can't apologize to him," Randy moaned.

"Why not?"

"I don't know what to say."

"Buy him a new fishbowl and a goldfish and knock on his door. Two words, Randy, that's all I ask—*I'm sorry*."

"But it's admitting it was all my fault."

His father sighed and shook his head.

"What's wrong?"

"We go through life pretending that somewhere a grand court is convened with every misunderstanding, and that it issues an official decision, 'He was in the wrong' or 'It wasn't his fault.' And we play out our life for that imaginary court, making our defense before it every day of our life, justifying our mistakes, minimizing our errors. Well, the court doesn't exist. And much of the heartache in the world comes, not only because of sin, but also because we hurt each other's feelings."

Randy thought about Mr. Janowski changing the water every night for the goldfish. Did he really talk to it?

"Randy, there's no loss to your manhood to say you're sorry. It's not even admitting guilt. Go ahead and learn to lessen the hurt of those around you. That's what the Savior would do—you know he would."

They pulled into the driveway and sat for a minute. Finally Randy grinned. "The pizza was just a plan to talk to me, wasn't it?"

His father laughed. "How can you argue with me when I'm paying ten dollars for you to gorge yourself?"

The next day after school Randy went to a store and asked the clerk for the happiest goldfish they had. After fifteen minutes of trying to please Randy, the clerk reached in with a net and pulled out a fish.

"This is the happiest one we have," he announced with an air of finality.

"Are you sure?"

"Trust me," the frustrated clerk said.

An hour later, Randy knocked on Mr. Janowski's door.

"I told you never to come back here again!" Mr. Janowski fumed.

Randy thrust out the new fishbowl with a goldfish swimming around in it.

"Mr. Janowski, I'm sorry."

He watched the anger melt on Mr. Janowski's face.

"Come in." They went inside. Mr. Janowski cleared off a place on top of the piano for the fishbowl, got some fish food, and scattered it in.

"I think I'll call him Otto."

"Otto—that's a good name. I think he looks happy."

"You're right. He is happy, isn't he?"

That night Randy knocked at another door. Michelle's father opened it and scowled. "What do you want?"

"I'm sorry," Randy said.

Mr. Reynolds looked at him strangely. "You came to apologize?"

"Yes, I'm sorry."

"Michelle," her father called out, "we have company."

When she showed up, he said it again. "I'm sorry."

She smiled warmly at him. He stayed for popcorn, and they invited him to go waterskiing with the family in the summer.

There's magic in some words, he thought as he walked home. *For instance, take the words* I'm sorry—*and also the word* Michelle.

As he walked home, he began to think.

The house was a raging inferno.

"Help!" Michelle cried out from a second-floor window . . .

Afterwards Refreshments Will Be Served

They met once a month at Bishop Taylor's home. The ward was small enough that they could cram all the sixteen- to eighteen-year-old youth into his living room.

Lisa Rodgers, Laurel class president, conducted the meeting. She welcomed everyone, called on someone to give the prayer, and then turned the time over to the bishop.

The bishop waited for the few lingering whispers to stop, then began. "We've been having these firesides for the past two years now. For the past several months we've had a planned program, but tonight I thought we'd just talk. I want each of you to tell me what you love most about the gospel of Jesus Christ." And with that he sat down.

The joking and teasing stopped, and then it was quiet.

The seconds ticked by. Bishop Taylor thought about trying to fill the silence, but seeing the thoughtful expressions on the faces of the youth in his ward, he decided the time was being put to good use.

1. Jason Miller

Jason fixed his gaze on the carpet below him. It had been only two months since he had started going back to Church after having been a runaway for four months. A lot can happen in four months when you're just going with the flow, doing whatever seems like a good idea at the time.

First published in the *New Era,* April 1987

He had done things he thought would make him happy—and yet, strangely enough, they eventually made him feel worse.

He had quit high school, left home, and moved in with some friends across town. One night late, after he'd been drinking, he was hit by a car as he tried to cross the street.

The next thing he remembered was the sound of a familiar voice. "I'm Jason Miller's mother. How is he?" she said to the nurse in intensive care.

"So far he's stable, but he's still unconscious."

"My husband will be coming soon. He was out of town when we got the news. I phoned him, and he'll be here in an hour. Is it okay if I stay here with my son?"

"Of course. I'll get you a chair."

Jason felt her hand on his. "Jason, I'm here."

"He can't hear you," the nurse said.

Jason could hear his mother, though. He just couldn't let her know. There was some kind of a barrier.

"Jason, I love you. I'm sorry about your accident. Everything is going to be okay. As soon as your dad gets here, he'll administer to you. He'll be here in just a short time." She paused. "Jason, you don't know how many times I've prayed for you. Every day, several times a day. I've prayed that when you grow tired of being rebellious, that you'll know we love you and come back. We made some mistakes as parents. Maybe we were too critical of you, too quick to find fault, but we did our best. There are some things we'd do differently now, but we did the best we could at the time.

"There's a story the Savior told—I've thought so much about it lately. A father had a son who wanted to be independent. He asked for his inheritance and took it to live in another town. He lived a wild life. But then there was a famine, and he ran out of money and was forced to get a job feeding swine. He was so hungry he thought about eating the husks he was feeding to the pigs. But then he thought about his father's servants, how much better off they were than he was. He decided to return home and ask his father if he could be just one of his servants.

"His father was in the field the day the son came home. The scriptures tell us he saw his son from afar off and ran out to greet him, and when he saw him, he threw his arms around him and welcomed him back and requested the servants to prepare a celebration dinner.

"I'll tell you a secret. It was no accident that the father saw his son from far off, because I think he looked down that road for his son many times every day. Like your father and I have. Sometimes we've left the lights on all night just in case you might come home during the night. We wanted you to know you were welcome, but you never came."

His mother broke down crying.

"I'm sorry. It's just that sometimes it's hard to be a parent. You'll find that out someday. It's hard to wait for a prodigal son to come home. We love you, Jason. All we want is what's best for you. Heavenly Father loves you. Jason, please, when you're able, come home. Live the gospel. It's not too late to come back."

Jason had heard everything his mother said, but he couldn't seem to make any movement to tell her.

Later Jason was aware that his father had come into the room with another man. He felt their hands being placed lightly on his head. And then they administered to him.

The next day Jason came out of his coma. A week later he was well enough to go home.

And now he was working with the bishop on plans to someday serve a mission.

Jason stood up, cleared his throat, and began his testimony. *"I'm glad Christ gave the parable of the prodigal son . . ."*

2. Lisa Rodgers

Lisa's family had moved to town two years ago. She was so outgoing and friendly that she soon had become accepted as one of the group, both in high school and in the Church.

But she hadn't always been the way she was now. In ninth grade, in another town, there had been some problems. She doubted if her parents were even aware of what they were. One night at a party some things had happened that never should have.

For the longest time, she had kept it covered up. Months drifted by. On the surface Lisa was the same as always, but on the inside, she worried that God had not forgiven her. She prayed every day for forgiveness.

But then one day the bishop gave her a birthday interview. She'd been in interviews before and had always managed to avoid talking about the thing which still troubled her. But in this interview, for some reason, the bishop made her aware of a scripture. Maybe she'd heard it before, but for some reason, this time it seemed to be just for her.

"Lisa, would you read this out loud?" the bishop had asked.

She read from the 58th section of the Doctrine and Covenants, verses 42-43: "Behold, he who has repented of his sins, the same is forgiven, and I, the Lord, remember them no more. By this ye may know if a man repenteth of his sins—behold, he will confess them and forsake them."

The scripture gave her the courage she needed to tell the bishop about what had happened, and with his counsel, she was eventually able to complete the steps of repentance. And now she knew for certain that the Lord had forgiven her, and she wasn't weighed down with guilt any longer. She would never forget how wonderful it was to feel all the guilt and shame being lifted off her shoulders, to feel that Father in heaven had accepted her repentance, and that the atonement of the Savior made it possible for her to be forgiven of the mistake she had made.

After that experience, lessons about the Savior became very important to her, for she knew that she herself owed so much to him for what he had done for her.

Lisa stood up. Nobody in the ward knew about her past. And she would never tell them either because it would serve no purpose. But there was one thing she wanted them to know about.

"I'm grateful that Jesus loved us enough to take upon him our sins and make it possible for us to repent . . ."

3. Todd Richards

Things had not been easy for Todd. He was the only member of the Church in his family. He had come in contact with the Church over a year ago through Lisa.

Lisa was the warmest, most enthusiastic, most Christ-centered person he had ever met. They were in student government together. He was president of the student senate and she was vice president. He'd spent many hours in her home, working on various student projects, and it was like being in heaven as far as he was concerned. Her mother always baked cookies for them when she knew they'd be meeting. And even if the house wasn't always perfectly neat, there was a good feeling there.

One day he had asked Lisa why she was so different, and she had told him about her membership in the Church. He was interested in what she had to say, and so she invited him to church. Soon he was taking the missionary lessons at her house.

In a month's time he was ready to get baptized. He asked his parents for permission. They had no religious preferences themselves, so they gave their permission and he was baptized.

A short time later, his uncle heard about what had happened, and he came all the way from Illinois to try to talk Todd out of being a Mormon.

After his uncle had spent half a day being critical of

the Church, his parents were finally persuaded to forbid Todd from attending church. No matter how much Todd complained, his parents would not budge. He could attend any other church, but not that church.

It's not fair, Todd thought. *I've never given my parents any trouble, and all I'm asking is for them to let me worship God in the way I want to.*

He considered pretending to go on a walk and then sneaking over to attend sacrament meeting. He phoned the bishop and asked for advice. The bishop told him to honor his parents and to set a good example and to try to win their confidence.

Todd followed the advice. At first it was hard to show love to his parents when they wouldn't let him do the thing he most wanted to do, but he worked on it. He quit talking back to them and tried to be someone they could depend on.

One day Lisa's family invited them over for a barbecue. It was good for his parents to see that Church members could be very nice people.

Just before Todd turned seventeen, his mother asked him what he wanted for his birthday. He said, "For you and Dad to go with me to church."

She looked at him closely. "Is it really that important to you?"

"Yes."

"All right, we'll do that as our birthday present to you."

Once his parents had gone to church, they softened in their opposition and let him attend. Sometimes they would even go with him, especially if he had a talk to give in sacrament meeting.

Todd stood up. *"I'm glad that Jesus has restored the Church back to the earth, and that he's given us men like our bishop to help us when we have problems . . ."*

4. Julie Bateman

Julie sat and listened to the others talk. She wondered if she would be able to say anything without crying. It would be difficult. But then she decided that maybe it didn't matter if she cried or not. These were her friends and they'd understand.

Above everything else, Julie was so glad to be alive. Each day when she woke up, she took delight in things she'd taken for granted before—the sun, the blue sky, the song of birds—it was such a wonderful world.

Julie was a senior. In two weeks she would graduate. Her senior year had been something she would never forget. She and her friends had been together all through school, and they realized that this was their last year to be together. They all wanted to have some good memories.

Julie had been in the pep club since she was a sophomore. She'd made some very good friends. Most of them weren't LDS, but they were still great friends. They respected her beliefs and didn't complain if she didn't drink when they all went out together after a game.

One day Vicky Kramer, her best friend since the eighth grade, talked to her. "Julie, after lunch tomorrow a bunch of us are going up to Daryl's cabin to have a party for all us seniors. Daryl's dammed off a section of the creek so we can go swimming. You'll come, won't you?"

"I don't know, Vicky," she began.

"I know what's bothering you. Okay, there will be a keg there, but we're getting diet soda especially for you. C'mon, we just want you to be with us. This is one of the last times we'll have to all be together. Please."

It was hard to say no to Vicky.

The afternoon with all the seniors had been a lot of fun. These were some of her best friends, and they all knew their time together was growing to a close. In the fall, they would scatter to colleges all across the country.

There was not just one keg, but two, and near the end of the party, there was still a lot left in one of the kegs. "C'mon, everybody, let's finish this up," someone kept saying.

Near midnight they decided to head back to town. Somehow Julie and Vicky got separated, and Vicky ended up in a car driven by Ross Turner, a senior basketball player who'd received a full-ride scholarship to the state university.

Julie was in the car driven by Bruce Seeley. Bruce had been one of the most eager to help finish up the last remaining dregs from the keg. "Bruce, why don't you let me drive?" Julie had asked.

"I can drive perfectly well."

"You've been drinking all day but I haven't. C'mon, it'll be safer."

"No girl can outdrive Bruce Seeley."

"She's right," someone said, "she's the one who should drive."

By this time the first car, the one driven by Ross, had already taken off. They switched places, and Julie got in the driver's seat.

"Did you ever hear the story," Bruce said, "that ends, 'You'd better drive. You're too drunk to sing'?"

It was a gravel road heading down a steep mountain canyon leading to home, so Julie drove slowly.

"It's going to take us forever to get down at this rate," Bruce said.

A few minutes later when they rounded a corner, they saw the first car. It had slid off a curve and hit a large tree. Vicky Kramer died in the accident.

Julie stood up, tears streaming down her cheeks. "*I'm so grateful to know that life goes on after we die. You all know about Vicky. Well, I miss her so much . . .*"

5. Craig Matthews

Craig didn't know what he was going to do or where

he would end up. That afternoon after church his mother had informed him that his parents were getting a divorce. His father would be moving back to Iowa. He could live with whichever parent he chose.

He had listened to her news and then asked, "Is that it, then?"

"Yes, that's it."

Craig had gone outside and ridden his ten-speed all afternoon, his feelings churning up inside him. He loved both his parents. How could he choose between them? What was he going to do? He never would have thought that his parents would get a divorce. They had even been married in the temple. Why would they want to break up after all these years? He had never felt so alone in his whole life. It was like his entire world was coming unglued.

At the fireside now, still in shock, he wiped a tear from his eye. Julie noticed, and reached over and touched his arm.

He wanted to tell how much her concern had meant to him. Right now he felt like his friends in the Church were the only thing he could count on. He loved them all so much. He knew some of them had had problems, and they had seemed to get through okay. Maybe if they all stuck together, he'd be able to get through this crisis.

He knew he couldn't stand up and say anything to the group, but he wished everyone in that room knew how much he loved them.

6. Chrissy Peterson

Chrissy Peterson had her arms folded neatly in front of her. She knew that some of the other girls were crying, but she wouldn't cry. I'm not like these others, she thought. I don't have a problem. I have everything under control. I get good grades in all my classes, I have a boyfriend, my weight's under control now, I got a superior rating on my piano solo, and I'm a National Merit Scholarship winner.

Everything's under control. I'm not like some of these others. Like Jason Miller. He really had a drinking problem. It's a miracle he's still alive.

I don't have a problem. Other people have problems but not me. There's nobody who's been able to achieve what I've done this year. In any area you pick I've done great.

But what am I going to do if they have refreshments? I can't eat anything or my weight will go up. All I've had today is a piece of toast, and that was just because my mother made me have breakfast. I weigh less than 100 pounds now. That's good progress. Another ten pounds or so ought to do it. And to think I used to weigh 128 pounds. I was so fat. It's funny that even though the scale says I weigh less, I still look fat.

Julie is crying and trying to talk at the same time. Doesn't she know how messy that looks? Somebody should at least give her a tissue so she can wipe her face.

I wish I could have refreshments. I guess I could. But then I'd feel guilty and maybe I'd go into their bathroom and throw it all up again. What I wish more than anything is that I could have refreshments without feeling guilty. Yesterday my mother said she thought I was anorexic. I don't have a problem though. She has a problem. Everything is going my way.

Now the bishop is talking. He's talking about the Savior. I wish he wouldn't talk like that. What does he mean, everybody has problems? Not me—I don't have any problems.

Who am I trying to kid? I have a problem, all right. Father in heaven, can you hear me think? I have a problem. I know it's not right, but I can't eat. I feel so weak all the time, trying to push myself all the time, trying to be perfect in everything. Oh Father, I can't do it. I'm crying now. Everybody can see me, but I don't care. I can't handle this anymore. I've got to ask my parents and the bishop to help me out of this. I think I'm going to die if I don't change the way I feel about food.

I do have a problem, and I can't handle it all by myself. I'll ask the bishop if I can talk to him right after the fireside. Oh Father, please help me, like you've helped the others.

The fireside came to a close. The things that were said came from the heart. Not everyone spoke, and sometimes what was not spoken, but only felt, contributed to the spirit of gratefulness for the gospel of Jesus Christ.

Life is not easy, but it is always better with the gospel of Jesus Christ.

Afterwards there were cookies and ice cream.

Letters from a Loving Brother

Dear Libby,

I guess you don't know me, but I'm Kevin's brother. I don't know if he ever mentioned me or not. Did he? My name is Rick. I'm fifteen.

I don't know if you know anything about me, but I know plenty about you. Are you worried? (That's a joke.) Kevin wrote a lot of neat things about you. I kept all his letters. I was reading them this morning. I like to go to his room and wrap his sleeping bag around me and read his letters.

In one of his letters he said your real name is Elizabeth, but you like Libby better. I do, too. Except it reminds me of canned green beans. He said you were the first Mormon he'd ever met.

I'm fifteen now. I was thirteen when Kevin joined the Marines, and fourteen when he was killed guarding the American Embassy in Rome.

Kevin and I were really close. Even my parents said so.

You probably didn't know it, but he told me a lot of things about you. He told me things he didn't even tell my parents. For instance, once he wrote and said that your hair is the same color as our dog. Now before you get mad, you should know we have an Irish setter named Lady, and the color of her hair is my favorite color. So if what Kevin said about your hair is true, then I think that when you get a

---

First published in the *New Era,* April 1986

little older you could be Miss America or even that lady on TV's "Wheel of Fortune." I like her because she doesn't talk much. Mainly she points at the prizes and smiles.

Kevin told me a lot of things about you. I know you're a dental assistant, and that's how he met you, when you were cleaning his teeth.

Personally if I were a dental assistant I'd never fall in love with one of my patients. In the first place, how can you stand to put your fingers in a stranger's mouth? And second, how can you respect somebody after you've scraped away all that crud from their teeth? I mean, it's like you know the absolute worst thing about them.

He said he looked up at you, and that you had the most beautiful eyes he'd ever seen in his life. Do many guys fall in love with you when you're scraping gunk off their teeth? I never would. No way. Of course Kevin always was a little different.

He also told me that on your first date you went jogging together. That sounds like Kevin. He was always looking for ways to save money. And that you didn't drink or smoke, but you were a lot of fun anyway. He said that made him curious about you. I guess that's why he agreed to go to your house and let those ministers from your church talk to him about God and stuff like that.

You must really be something to get him to change religions, because I thought he was pretty good the way he was. And I guess it's no secret that it set my parents off. Mom said she thought you probably sweet-talked him into it. She says things like *sweet-talk* all the time because she's from Georgia. She has all these strange sayings that none of the rest of us have ever heard before.

But about you sweet-talking him into becoming a Mormon—I don't think so, because Kevin could be pretty stubborn sometimes, and if it's true what Kevin said about you not kissing him for a long time after he started dating you, then I don't think anybody can say you sweet-talked him into anything.

I didn't mind Kevin joining your church if that's what he wanted to do.

By now you're probably wondering why I'm writing this letter. Actually it's mainly because Dr. Nelson asked me to do it. He's the psychologist assigned to my case. I told him about you and he told me to write you a letter. He gave me a week to do it, and the week's up tomorrow, and I have to go back to him then, so I'm sitting here in Kevin's room, with his sleeping bag wrapped around me, writing you. It's very early in the morning. Actually it's three-thirty. Sometimes I can't sleep at night.

I was fourteen when he was killed. I wonder sometimes what was so valuable in that embassy. A bunch of old men? Was any of it worth Kevin's life?

He sent me pictures of Italy. I've got one of him standing by an old boat. He's smiling in the picture, and there's this beautiful blue water behind him. The picture was taken just a month before he died.

It makes me wonder if at the same time the picture was taken, somebody was meeting in some little room, maybe in one of those houses in the background of that picture, working out a plan to bomb the American embassy.

Besides being my brother, Kevin was my best friend. Some people said they'd never seen two brothers so close. Even when he was away from home, he wrote to me about things that were happening to him.

He liked to kid around even in his letters. In one letter he'd give me a puzzle, and in the next letter he'd answer it. It used to drive me crazy sometimes. But he was like that. Always fun.

I saved all his letters. I read them every night.

If a guy could have any kind of brother, he'd be the one

to choose. To me he was the kind of guy who can do anything. He made me a kite once after I'd broken mine. He just made it out of newspaper and some branches from a tree. Did you know he got freckles on his face in the summer? He was never ashamed to tell people I was his younger brother. Once he even took me along on one of his dates. We went to a carnival, and he let me ride with him and his girlfriend on the Ferris wheel, in the same car. It was a little crowded, but he didn't seem to mind.

Once he took me camping, just the two of us. During the night there was this heavy thunderstorm. It didn't last long, but my sleeping bag got wet. His was dry because he'd remembered to put down a ground cloth. He told me to do it too when we set up camp, but I said it was too much bother. The reason I said that was because the sky was clear then.

Well, after the storm, and my sleeping bag was wet, he didn't get mad and tell me it was my fault anyway for not putting down a ground cloth. Instead he got out of his sleeping bag and asked me to get in it instead. I asked him what he was going to do, and he said he thought he'd go build a fire and think.

I let him do it because I was too young to realize that it was only two-thirty in the morning and nobody in their right mind goes out and sits by a fire for four hours in the middle of the night to think.

He did things like that for me all the time.

All the girls loved him. They really did. In high school for sure, because I was around and saw what was happening around our house. I wish I had a dime for every girl who came over to our house with a batch of cookies for Kevin. It was good for me too, because he'd always share with me.

Did you love him? A lot? I hope you did.

I asked him once why girls liked him so much, and he said it was because he treated them right. I asked him what he meant, and he said you've got to remember one thing about girls and that is that they're people too. And I said well of course they are. Everybody knows that. So he named this really foxy movie star, and asked me if I thought anybody knew what her favorite color was. And I said no. And he said, that's because people don't treat her like she's a person. What do they treat her like, I asked, and he said they treat her like she's a toy.

You can't do that, he said. You've got to find out interesting things about them, like if they ever had measles, or when's the last time they used crayons to draw a picture, or if they've ever baked a pecan pie, or if they play the piano, or if they know how to change the oil in a car.

This is really getting to be a long letter, isn't it? Well, I'm almost through.

I have a question I want to ask you. I read all his letters this morning. And mostly I understand them all, except the last one, the one he wrote just before he was killed.

And that's the main reason why I wanted to write you. I'll copy down part of his last letter for you. I'll skip the parts you wouldn't be interested in.

I heard yesterday that an embassy in Germany was bombed. I hope they stay away from ours. Sometimes I get scared.

Rick, here's a puzzle for you. Ready? When things get bad and I'm afraid, I turn to another brother of ours. He's faced it all before. When I get to a place in my life where I need help with a certain thing, then I read his words and they help me.

You and I are real close, and I've never really preached to you much, but I wanted to tell you about this older brother of ours. He's someone I can go to for advice, and he will be there for you too. Because he's been here on earth before us, and he knows the best way for us to live. And he loves us, even more than I love you.

In my next letter I'll tell you who this brother is. And where you can find the things to read he wants to tell you.

Love, Kevin.

That's what he wrote. And that's the thing I can't understand.

Here I am, after he's dead, reading his letters over and over again, trying to understand more about him. And then to think that he was doing the same thing about a brother of his.

But the thing that doesn't make sense is that there is no other brother. There's just the two of us in our family. So what did he mean? When the army sent all his belongings back to us, I went through everything, hoping to find what he said he had from this other brother that he talked about. But there weren't any other letters except the ones from me and my parents and you—just that, and an old beat-up copy of the Bible and the book of the Mormons.

What I want to know is—who is this other brother he talked about? And where are the letters from this other brother to Kevin that he said he read all the time? I need to know because I really need help now too, at least that's what my parents and Dr. Nelson think.

My mother just came in and told me it was late and I should go to bed. I told her I was writing a letter to you. She told me that you came to the funeral. I'm sorry I wasn't there to meet you then. I'm sorry I ran away and caused my parents more worry. But I'm all right now.

If you have any ideas on my question, please write to me. And would it be all right if we wrote to each other once in a while? Kevin loved you, so you must feel bad too. Maybe we can help each other for a while, and then I won't have to keep going back to Dr. Nelson.

Your new friend (I hope),
Rick

Lookin' Good

"Did anyone work problem number 12?" Mr. Bentley asked the class.

The students all shook their heads. Except for Jeff. He raised his hand and said, "I did."

"Oh?" Mr. Bentley said with raised eyebrows. "What did you get for your answer?"

"(X-Y)/(X+Y)."

Mr. Bentley looked at him strangely. "That's what I got too. Did anyone else work it?"

Silence.

Mr. Bentley looked at Jeff with newfound respect. "It's a hard problem. Did it take you very long?"

He modestly shrugged his shoulders. "Not really."

"Would you like to show the class how you got your answer?"

"No, that's all right. You go ahead."

He was a senior in high school. His family had just moved to town because his father was the new superintendent of schools. The reason he appeared so bright in math was because he'd used his dad's stationery and written the publisher for the teacher's supplement that had all the problems worked out.

After putting the problem on the board, Mr. Bentley turned to Jeff and asked, "Is that how you did it?"

First published in the *New Era,* November 1984

Jeff casually nodded his head. "More or less."

The class bell rang, and it was time for lunch. He ate alone. He didn't care. There was nobody in this town he wanted to know anyway.

When school was over he went downtown and continued to look for a job.

A week later he found a job at an expensive men's clothing store. He worked after school and on Saturdays. They didn't actually let him sell anything; he unpacked clothing, cleaned the rest rooms, dusted, and ran errands.

Upstairs the store was mahogany and marble, but in the store's basement there was no need for a good impression because no customers ever ventured that far. Alterations were made in the basement, and there was a large steam press that hissed clouds of steam. The two women who worked there were grumpy and were always complaining about everyone else.

Beyond the alterations room was an entire area full of mannequin parts—a bin for heads, and another for arms. And scattered along the dimly lit hall stood headless, armless, bronzed torsos on the roughened cement floor.

Another section was filled with remnants of past window displays—signs that define for people what the "Man of Action" is wearing. But the "Man of Action" changes every season, and the signs were for last year, so they lay in stacks gathering dust, waiting for the window man to finally decide what to keep and what to throw away.

Jeff spent much of his workday in the basement. Starting from cardboard slabs he made up suit and tie and sock boxes. He also mailed altered suits to out-of-town customers. Also it was in the basement where they kept the supplies for polishing and dusting the mahogany upstairs.

One day he walked to the end of the dreary hallway. The lighting was bad and the clutter more evident as he proceeded.

What a mess, he thought. He moved aside a sign and saw a stack of men's magazines. He was embarrassed by the cover on top. Making sure nobody was around, he opened it up and quickly thumbed through its pages. There was a centerfold.

I've got no business looking at this, he thought, closing it and walking away.

Four days passed, and he never returned to the magazines. He congratulated himself on his self-control.

But one day he returned. It was a day when it seemed as if the world was against him. At breakfast his parents scolded him for driving the car but never putting any gas in it. His dad warned him that he'd better spend more time studying if he ever expected to get a college scholarship. At school he said hello to a girl, but she looked coolly at him as if he weren't even there.

He forgot the combination to his locker and had to go to the principal's office to ask for it. The girl working there smirked and suggested he write it on his hand so he wouldn't forget it. He flunked a world history exam. After school his boss yelled at him as soon as he walked in because two days ago he'd switched two suits and sent an old suit to a state senator who'd bought one especially for a press conference.

On that day, when the world seemed to be tumbling down on him, he found himself in the basement lifting up the old signs to again gaze at the stack of magazines.

Life was the same dull routine day after day. Besides that, nobody really cared about him anyway. What good did it do to try to live right when things just turn out rotten anyway?

He picked one of the magazines from the bottom of the stack and quickly stuffed it in his school notebook and walked away.

Later that night, at home, after family prayer, when his mom had embarrassed him by insisting on a good-night kiss, he went to his room and closed the door and read the magazine from cover to cover.

The next day at work he returned it to the bottom of the stack, and nobody was any the wiser. It was his little secret.

Over the course of the next two weeks, in the same way, he read every magazine in the stack. *It doesn't matter,* he thought. *I'm still the same. It hasn't affected me at all.*

Shortly after, he met Holly. She was from a small LDS branch in a town fifty miles away. She was a sophomore and he was a senior, and they met at a seminary Super Saturday. She had blonde hair and blue-green eyes. Her high cheekbones made everything about her face seem more dramatic. Her laughter reminded him of wind chimes.

After the first scripture chase, he sat behind her so he could watch her every move.

After the lesson, they all went to the gym to play volleyball. He stood next to her. Before the game started, she turned to him, smiled, and said, "You're new, aren't you?"

They talked. He couldn't remember what he said, because he was so anxious to have her like him. The game started and they lost, but he didn't care because she said she enjoyed getting to know him and that she hoped to see him again sometime.

When it was all over, he walked her outside to her parents' car. He asked her if he could come up and visit her sometime, and she said she'd like that.

"Do you think we'll be good friends?" she asked.

"I hope so."

"I do too."

He asked her for a picture, and she said she'd mail one to him.

On Monday of the next week, his math teacher asked him to sign up for the special college preparatory exam because if he did really well he could get a scholarship next year and anyone as bright as he was should be able to get a full-ride scholarship anywhere in the country.

"I'm not that smart," Jeff said.

"I think you're too modest. I've noticed the way you do all the homework. You're the best student I've ever had. I insist you take the exam."

Monday afternoon Holly's picture came in the mail. He sat at his desk and looked at it and dreamed that they'd fall in love and that someday she'd let him kiss her.

He phoned and thanked her for the picture.

"I hope we can be good friends," she said.

"Me too."

"Can I tell you something? Last summer I met this guy and we really got along well and it was the first guy I'd ever really dated. But after the second date he just quit. He didn't ever call me or say what was wrong. I figured it was probably something that I'd said. Of course my parents said not to worry, but that's what they say about everything."

"He was a fool to quit dating you," Jeff said.

She smiled. "Thanks, I needed that."

He took the standardized math exam, but he didn't do as well as people expected. "I think I had the flu that day," he explained to Mr. Bentley when the results came in.

He checked the magazine pile every week. Another new issue appeared on top of the pile. He told himself he wouldn't read it, but after a few days he broke down and did. He always promised himself it was the last. Somehow promising himself made him feel better.

Another Super Saturday rolled around again. He sat next to Holly in class. Afterwards everyone went roller skating. He skated with her the whole time. He asked her if she'd go with him to the junior-senior prom, and she said yes.

The next week Mr. Bentley asked to speak to him privately. "I don't understand how you can do so well on homework and so poorly on the hour exams."

"I get nervous taking exams," Jeff said.

"Is that the real reason?" Mr. Bentley asked.

The junior-senior prom came. Holly had made arrangements to stay with Church members in town.

After the dance he drove out to a country lane and parked. He kissed her for the first time. He kissed her again. Suddenly, uninvited, came a flood of images from the magazines. He didn't like the thoughts racing through his mind. He tried to make them go away, but they wouldn't.

Suddenly he was afraid of himself around Holly. He started the car and drove to where she was staying the night.

"Is anything wrong?" she asked.

He felt terrible. He realized that if she knew what he'd been thinking, she would hate him. "I'd better go now. Good night."

"What did I do wrong?" she asked him.

"Nothing," he said.

"You won't ever call me again, will you? What's wrong with me? At least tell me that."

"It's me. There's something wrong with me."

As he drove home, he hated himself. He decided not to date her anymore because of what he might do if he listened to the thoughts put there from the magazines. He promised himself not to read the magazines anymore, but he did. They didn't demand much from him except that he turn the pages.

One day Mr. Bentley called him in after class. "I think you've been cheating on the homework, but I can't prove it. For your own sake, if you have, then admit it. No class is worth damaging your integrity over. Just confess what you've been doing, and I won't flunk you. I'll give you a C—a good, clean, honestly earned C."

"I don't know what you're talking about."

Mr. Bentley had to give him a B because there was no proof.

Graduation day finally came. Jeff came down with the flu and asked to be excused from commencement. It was better that way.

Throughout the summer his father kept asking him to apply for college, but he didn't feel like it.

One Sunday his Sunday School teacher told him he'd been chosen in the premortal existence to be alive at this time to help prepare for the second coming of the Savior.

She doesn't know me, he thought. *She doesn't know the way I really am. Nobody does.*

His bishop asked him to get ready for a mission, but Jeff knew he wasn't that kind of a guy. He had no plans.

One Sunday in July, his bishop asked to speak to him in his office. The bishop talked about Jeff's being made an elder. Rather than have to explain why he didn't want to be an elder, Jeff went along with the idea. The bishop gave Jeff an interview. It started out easy enough, but before Jeff knew it the bishop was in deep waters. Jeff wasn't ready to confess. So he lied.

Perhaps because he had no reason to suspect any misconduct, the bishop wasn't as penetrating with his questions as he should have been. When it was over, he told Jeff he'd passed the interview. "Stake conference is next Sunday. We'll see you then. Your parents will be proud of you. Now the only thing you have to do is go see the stake president."

"What for?" he asked.

"He needs to interview you too."

The executive secretary had set up all the interviews on Sunday after church, but he'd set them too close together, so there was a line of people waiting to get in. Two of the guys from his ward, also graduating seniors, were also in line.

Holly and her father showed up in the hallway too because her father had a meeting to go to.

"Is it all right if I stand next to you in line?" she asked.

"I guess so."

He looked at her. She was more beautiful than he'd remembered.

"What are your plans now that you've graduated?" she asked.

"I'm not sure."

"I hope you go on a mission," she said.

"Why?"

"I know you'd make a great missionary."

He shook his head. "I doubt it."

She touched him on the sleeve. "You've got to have faith in yourself. I think you're . . . special."

He shook his head. "No, I'm not."

"There you go again."

He couldn't look her in the face because she reminded him of what could have been.

"You quit coming to Super Saturdays."

"Yeah," he said.

"Why?"

"I got busy."

"I wished you hadn't been so busy," she said quietly. "But I learned from it."

"What did you learn?"

"That you can't depend on other people to make you feel good about yourself. It's got to be inside you."

For a moment he allowed himself the luxury of looking into her eyes. She was not afraid anymore. He looked away.

The next person in line went into the stake president's office.

"Did you pass?" someone asked the one coming out.

"What do you think?"

"I doubt it, but hey, if you can pass, anybody can."

They all laughed.

Jeff's face turned bright red because he was next in line.

"Is something wrong?" she asked.

"No, why?"

"Your face is so red. Do you have a fever?"

"Yeah, I guess I do. You'd better stay away from me."

She smiled. "I'll take the chance it's not contagious."

"I hope it isn't."

Several minutes passed. He turned to her and said quietly, "I have a problem."

"What kind of a problem?"

"I can't tell you."

"You need to tell someone. You can't keep a problem to yourself."

The door opened again. President Rossiter came out and shook Jeff's hand and asked him in. They went through the same questions again, and again he lied just as he had to the bishop.

When they were finished, President Rossiter looked uneasy.

"Is something wrong?" Jeff asked.

"I'm not sure. Maybe you'd better tell me."

"What?"

"I just don't feel good about what you've said."

Jeff wiped his forehead.

"Let me explain something, Jeff. You could probably lie to me or your bishop and get away with it. We're only human, and we might never know the difference. But when I ask these questions, I represent the Lord as if he were asking them, and if you don't tell the truth, then it's as if you're lying to the Lord. Now let's go over some of the questions one more time."

They went over the questions one by one. Again Jeff lied, but by the time the questions were over his face was dripping with sweat.

President Rossiter shook his head. "I'm sorry, but there's something wrong. Would you like to talk about it?"

Jeff shook his head. "There's all those people waiting in the hall. If you take too much time with me, they'll know there's something wrong."

"Telling the truth doesn't take any longer than lying does."

Jeff sat there stonefaced.

"God knows what the problem is. Let me know too, so I can help you with whatever it is. You are important in his eyes. He reserved you to come to earth at this time to help bring about the Second Coming."

Jeff shook his head. "I wish people would quit saying that. It's not true about me. You don't know me. Nobody knows what I'm really like."

"Then why don't you tell me," President Rossiter said quietly.

"All right, I will. I lied to my bishop, and I lied to you. I've cheated in school, and I've read magazines. Bad magazines. Don't tell me to stop. I've tried that, but no matter how hard I try, I'm just not strong enough anymore. It's like it's got control over me, and no matter how hard I say to myself I won't ever do it again, I can't stop. How can you possibly know what it's like? I'm not like any of the people waiting in the hall out there. I've got a dirty mind."

He tried to make the shame come out quietly, but it didn't. It was the first time he'd cried since he was six years old. *So now,* he thought bitterly, *on top of everything else, I'm not even a man, and everyone in the hall knows it because they can hear me crying.*

President Rossiter put his arm around his shoulder. Jeff wondered if he'd talk about this in stake conference, and if after that people would stand in the halls and secretly smirk as he walked by.

He asked President Rossiter about it. "I don't tell anyone, Jeff, not anyone."

Jeff finally opened up and told it all—about the magazines and the thoughts that wouldn't go away, and about cheating on homework, and about all the lying he'd done to cover it all up. He told every secret thing he'd done until it was all out in the open, and there was nothing left to hide. When he was finished, he asked, "Will you excommunicate me now?"

"Jeff, your bishop and I are going to work with you to help you repent, so you can wipe the slate clean again."

Jeff looked up. "I can start over?"

"If you repent, you can. Your bishop will outline some steps to follow."

"But I've disappointed the Lord."

"Yes, you have."

"But how can he forgive me for what I've done?"

"Because he loves you."

"And if I do, someday will I be able to be an elder and go on a mission?"

"Yes, but it's up to you. You can be forgiven if you turn from your sins and repent."

"But what about the bad thoughts?"

"Replace them with good ones."

Half an hour later he walked out into the hall again.

"It's about time," one of his high school friends complained. "What were you two talking about in there?"

President Rossiter smiled. "Bob, come on in and find out for yourself."

Jeff started down the hall. He walked past Holly. He turned away. He didn't want her to see his eyes because they were bloodshot from crying.

"Are you all right?" she called out after him.

He stopped walking and turned around to face her. "Yeah, I'm fine."

"Can I walk with you?" she asked.

He smiled at her. "I'd really like that."

The next day at work he put all the magazines into a

box and lugged it up to the floor with the mahogany and marble.

The store was momentarily without customers.

"Hey, do these magazines belong to anyone?" he announced loudly.

All the salesmen came up to the counter where he'd set the box. They looked at the box full of tattered, dusty magazines. One by one they all denied that the magazines belonged to them.

"If they don't belong to anyone, I guess nobody will mind if I just toss 'em out, right?" Nobody objected.

He went outside and dumped them in a trash can just in time to see the garbage truck coming down the alley.

The hydraulic ram on the garbage truck crushed the box and mixed it with other garbage collected on the block—wilted brown lettuce and old potato and carrot peelings and a large pail of darkened, deep-fat grease from the restaurant next door.

On his way inside again, he started whistling a hymn to himself. He decided he'd call Holly after work and ask if she'd go with their family on a picnic next week out at the lake. Maybe he could teach her how to water-ski.

Inside again, he passed a mirror customers used to look at themselves when they tried out clothes for the "Man of Action." He smiled at his reflection in the mirror. He liked what he saw.

And When the Night Came

It was eleven o'clock at night. Elder Todd Bradford lay in bed, listening to the slow, even breathing of his companion as he slept across the room.

What had gone wrong? For as long as he could remember, Todd had always known the right thing to say. *Polished* was the word people used when talking about Todd.

But even from the beginning of his mission, he'd felt as if he didn't belong. As if he were just going through the motions, copying what the other missionaries did, pretending he was like them. But he wasn't, and he knew it.

They said they knew the Church was true. He said it too, but sometimes he wasn't sure if he knew or not.

They said they knew Joseph Smith was a prophet of God, but sometimes he wondered if it was just because they'd been conditioned to say that since they were kids in Primary.

He was smart, he learned fast, he quickly learned to imitate the other missionaries. There'd even been some baptisms.

He'd gotten by all right for ten months. Until today. When they'd been tracting door-to-door. Todd's companion was Elder Stewart, who'd been in the mission field for only two weeks.

The first door was opened by someone not much older than Todd, wearing blue cotton slacks, and a short-sleeved

---

First published in the *New Era,* December 1985

sport shirt. He had a tanned face and athletic build and an easy, infectious smile. They introduced themselves. His name was Devin Ostler.

"What do you do?" Todd asked.

"I'm at the university," Devin answered.

"Taking classes?"

"No," Devin smiled. "Giving them."

"You're a professor?"

"That's what they say."

"You seem so young."

"Well, I guess I'm what they call a child prodigy. I'm twenty and have a doctorate in philosophy. C'mon in."

"Was that your car we saw coming in? The Corvette?"

"Yes, that's mine. Why?"

"I always wanted to have a red Corvette."

"Take it for a test ride if you want."

"Really?" Todd said. And then he noticed his companion looking strangely at him. "Well, no, I guess not," Todd continued. "We'd better just tell you why we're here."

Todd began to talk about their message. Devin listened with interest. When they finished, he asked with a smile, "You don't really believe that, do you?"

"Why not?"

"It seems so bizarre, that's all. Tell me, do you have any proof of what you say? Where are the gold plates these days?"

"The angel took them back."

"Sure he did," Devin laughed. "Really, guys, let's be honest with each other. I don't mind you going around looking for members, but no person with an education over the third grade could possibly swallow that story. Do you?" He was looking at Todd.

"I wouldn't be here unless I believed it," Todd said, mainly because he'd heard other missionaries say that.

Devin to answer the door. A beautiful blonde stood

there wearing a red jump suit that was so flashy it looked like it must be battery operated. Devin introduced the elders. Her name was Brandi.

"Oh, how about that!" she chirped, "You both have the same first name."

They just looked at each other and smiled.

"Devin, let's invite them to the party tonight," Brandi said.

"Sounds like a good idea," Devin said.

"It's at a friend's apartment, but they won't mind a couple more coming along." She gave the address.

"Hey, that's just across from our apartment," Todd said.

"Great, we'll see you then. It'll be a lot of fun," Brandi said.

"I don't think we'll be able to go," Elder Stewart said.

A few minutes later they left and continued tracting. Ten minutes later they met Sloan Thomas, a saintly looking elderly man who was the minister at a local congregation.

"How old do I look to you?" he asked them as he ushered them into his home.

"I don't know. Maybe forty-five," Elder Stewart said.

"I'm sixty-four. God has been good to me. Now you boys go ahead and present your message."

When they finished, Reverend Thomas looked Todd in the eye. "I've spent my entire life preaching the gospel. Every waking hour I've had a prayer in my heart to be an instrument in God's hand. He's answered my prayers. I love Jesus with all my heart. And so what you say bothers me. Do you mean to tell me that what I've done my entire life is wrong?"

"Well, I'm sure you've done the best you could do," Todd mumbled.

"Are you telling me that what I've said about Christ is wrong? For forty years I've preached that if you'll just accept Christ as your personal Savior, then you'll be saved in the kingdom of God. What can possibly be wrong with that?"

"Nothing really," Todd stammered.

"Except a person needs to be baptized by someone who has authority," Elder Stewart said.

"And you're saying that all these years I haven't had any authority?"

"That's right," Elder Stewart said.

Reverend Thomas turned to Todd. "If God didn't approve of what I was doing for the past forty years, why wouldn't he let me know?"

"He is now. That's why we're here," Elder Stewart said. "We have more truth to tell you about."

"More truth? What do you mean?"

"We have the Book of Mormon in addition to the Bible."

"All a person needs is found in the Bible. We don't need anything else."

They discussed back and forth. Todd could see that Reverend Thomas was as good a man as anyone he'd ever met. How can you tell a man like that, with love and warmth in his eyes, and a face like a prophet, that he's been wrong for forty years of his life?

"Boys," Reverend Thomas concluded, "I admire you for leaving your homes to come here to talk to people, but the truth is that the claims of your church are wrong. Mormons are simply not Christian. You are promoting lies by what you're doing, and my advice to you is pack up and go home."

For the first time in his life, Todd didn't know what he was supposed to say. They excused themselves and left. After that, for the rest of the afternoon, Todd just went through the motions.

That night they had two appointments, but much to Todd's relief, they both fell through.

He and Elder Stewart returned to their tiny apartment, got ready for bed, and said their prayers. Todd asked his companion to say the prayer.

And now Todd lay in bed and listened to his companion sleep.

He could hear music. He got up out of bed and looked out the window and across the street where the party was. The people had left their curtains open, and he could see right into the room. They were not much older than he was. They looked like people he'd like.

A red Corvette pulled up. Devin and Brandi got out and went up the sidewalk to the apartment building where the party was. Brandi looked terrific even from across the street, and he could hear her laughter as they walked.

Todd had always hoped that someday he'd have a girlfriend who looked like Brandi, except maybe a little more intelligent.

If I had a red Corvette, he thought, then girls like Brandi would go out with me too. Maybe someday, when I get off my mission. But if I'd just taken the money I'd saved for my mission, I could have put down a sizable down payment on a Corvette. Then, on a night like tonight, instead of standing here, I could be like Devin, at a party, talking with friends, with a girl like Brandi by my side.

What am I doing here? I don't belong here. And what if Reverend Thomas is right? What if all that we tell people is wrong? Suddenly it seemed to him that he'd spent his whole life living up to someone else's expectations, doing what someone else wanted him to do.

Even when he was six years old, he got up month after month and bore his testimony in church, always saying that he knew the gospel was true. What does it mean to say I know something is true? How can anyone know anything for sure? All this time I've been faking it. I don't belong here. Not me. How can I convert someone when I'm not sure myself?

He closed his eyes. God, help me. Please help me, he began.

A few minutes passed. When he opened his eyes, the first thing he saw was Devin and Brandi out on the veranda of the apartment across the way. They were in a deep, passionate embrace.

He felt that was an odd way for God to answer his prayer. Watching them carry on was more than Todd could stand, so he got up and went into the kitchen.

He looked up at the one overhead light on the ceiling. It made the room look like a morgue. He made himself a peanut butter sandwich and got a carton of milk and sat down at the table, but then he decided he wasn't hungry.

I'll go home, he thought, and take the money I have left and buy me a red Corvette, and then I'll be like Devin and find me a girl like Brandi too.

It was as if he were seeing everything for the first time, and everything was tinged with gray and dust. On the table was the jar of peanut butter, a knife still coated with peanut butter, and a sandwich made with the cheapest white bread that money could buy. Near the middle of the table, off to one side, was a stack of mission newsletters that nobody had thrown out for months. And just to the right of that was a crumpled paperback copy of the Book of Mormon that some unknown elder in the past had read while eating breakfast.

Todd picked up the book and examined it. As he turned the pages, he noticed that because it had been read during meals, some of the pages were stuck together.

In a way the glue from the food made it more of a challenge to read. He found one section of the book that was stuck together. He pried open a page in 2 Nephi, chapter 33, and began reading. "And now, my beloved brethren, and also Jew, and all ye ends of the earth, hearken unto these words and believe in Christ; and if ye believe not in these words believe in Christ. And if ye shall believe in Christ ye will believe in these words, for they are the words of Christ, and he hath given them unto me; and they teach all men that they should do good.

"And if they are not the words of Christ, judge ye—for Christ will show unto you, with power and great glory, that they are his words, at the last day" (verses 10-11).

Todd stopped reading. How odd that the very page he picked was one that testified of Christ. How could anyone reading that say that Mormons aren't Christian, he thought.

He picked another page at random and found on that one page alone there were five references to the Savior. And on another page, eleven references. And on another page, exact quotes from the Savior in the New World after his resurrection.

A little later he pried open the part of the book containing 3 Nephi. He began reading in chapter 11 about the Savior's appearance to the people in the New World. For the first time in his life, he could see it all in his mind. Jesus, coming down from heaven, his arms outstretched, the wound marks on his hands and feet. He speaks and his voice is gentle, but at the same time, it touches the very souls of those who hear him. "Behold, I am Jesus Christ, whom the prophets testified shall come into the world. And behold, I am the light and the life of the world" (verses 10-11).

He continued to read through much of the night. Suddenly passages seemed to jump out at him. Passages of scripture that answered the doubt and uncertainty of his heart.

He smiled a little when he read 3 Nephi 13:19-21: "Lay not up for yourselves treasures upon earth, where moth and rust doth corrupt, and thieves break through and steal; but lay up for yourselves treasures in heaven, where neither moth nor rust doth corrupt, and where thieves do not break through nor steal. For where your treasure is, there will your heart be also."

He smiled that he'd thought a red Corvette was more important than a mission. The Savior was talking about him, all right.

It wasn't the first time he'd read the scriptures. He'd read them in seminary, but mainly to find the answers to the teacher's questions. He'd read them in missionary study class, but mainly to be doing the assignment so he could check it off as being done. This was the first time the scriptures had become his scriptures, advice for him.

It seemed that the more he read, the lighter and more cheery the room became, until for the first time in his life, he realized he knew for a certainty that what he'd read was true. Now he knew that he'd stay on his mission and tell anyone, everyone who'd listen, about the truths found in the Book of Mormon.

He went into the bedroom and looked out the window. Across the street, the party was just now beginning to break up. Devin and Brandi slowly made their way to their car. Brandi lurched unsteadily, leaning precariously as Devin, not too steady himself, tried to help her.

Even so, Todd thought, she's still very attractive. And he continued to think that until she bent over and vomited all over a rose bush.

A minute later they made it to the car. Devin got in and tried to start it up. After several tries, it became apparent the car was not going to start. "Stupid idiotic car!" Devin raged, getting out and kicking the tires.

Todd started laughing. Strange, he thought, that Jesus would know so much about red Corvettes.

He lay down in bed and hoped he'd be able to get some sleep before the alarm went off. It would be another full day for him and his companion.

"Father in heaven," he prayed silently, "thanks for giving us the scriptures."

A Chance to Make Good

Ryan woke up at five that morning, anxious about his first day of work. After shaving and taking a shower in the bathroom adjoining the guest bedroom, he got dressed in the gray work slacks and shirt he had bought, purposely made dirty, and washed the day before. No use looking like a new worker, he had reasoned. Besides, his future father-in-law had suggested that he try to dress as much like the others as possible. They're all good boys, he had explained to Ryan, but sometimes they can make it rough on people who are different from themselves. Try to fit in, to be as much like them as possible, and you won't have any trouble.

He sat in the bedroom and watched the clock move slowly to six. Then, deciding he probably wouldn't wake up the others if he were quiet, he padded silently down the hall through the large dining room with the massive oak dining table into the large kitchen and then out on the patio. Sitting down at a table overlooking the swimming pool, he watched the Southern morning spread across the lush green mountains—a contrast to the elephant-hide browns of his Wyoming hills.

Kim's father was the next one up. He came out on the patio to sit with Ryan. "How'd you sleep?"

"Fine."

First published in the *New Era,* January 1985

"Good," he said, brushing a large hand over his bald scalp. "No one else is up. I guess breakfast is up to me."

"No, don't bother. I can wait. It's still early."

"I'd better warn you," he said with a smile, "Kim likes to sleep in, so if you're marrying her with the idea of having her fix you breakfast, you'd better think it over."

Ryan grinned, "I hadn't even thought about it."

"I suppose not. You're both too much in love to be very practical. If you'd been practical, you both wouldn't have fallen in love with someone who lives fifteen hundred miles from your homes. I can't understand it," he teased. "I sent Kim to Ricks College, after she joined your church, to get an education. Instead she got you."

"I reckon she got a good deal," Ryan grinned, purposely adding his cowboy drawl. "They say a good man is hard to find."

"Yes, that's what they say," Kim's father said, suddenly serious, "and I think Kim has found a good one. Let me get you some orange juice and me some coffee . . . that is, unless you can convert me in the next five minutes."

In a few minutes he was back with a tray. He set it down and returned with two slices of toast and a file of paperwork he constantly carried around with him. "Are you worried about today?" he asked Ryan.

"I guess a little."

"I'm in an awkward position too, you know," he said with a grin. "It's true you're going to marry my only child, and that I got you a job at the plant, and that I hope someday you'll take it over and run it so I can retire—but I wouldn't want anyone accusing me of being partial to you."

"I'm not afraid of hard work," Ryan said seriously.

"I'm sure you'll do well," he said, pushing the file folder away from him. "In a way I was serious about not playing favorites. I've told one of my supervisors to put you wherever he needs you. I don't plan to interfere. You'll be on your own. Is that acceptable to you?"

"It's the way I'd prefer it," Ryan said firmly.

A few minutes later, Kim came out, wearing a robe over her nightgown.

"Kimberly," her father gently scolded, "you shouldn't be out here with just a robe on."

"Why not? It's very modest."

"Seeing a woman before she's done herself up can be a rude shock. Maybe Ryan will change his mind about marrying you."

"Daddy," she drawled with a purposely thick Southern accent, "you're such a tease."

"I think she looks good—even in the morning," Ryan defended.

"See there, smarty?" Kim lightly countered. "He thinks I'm a natural beauty, a regular Southern rose."

"Okay, Rose," her father concluded, lovingly touching her arm, "how about cooking us some breakfast?"

"Slave driver," she protested with a smile and a hug.

While Kim cooked bacon and eggs, her father huddled over his stack of reports.

"Paperwork!" he growled, shaking his head in disgust. "It's all I ever do. You know, when I was your age and just starting out, it was fun. I had my own small welding shop, and I did all my own work. If it hadn't been for the development of nuclear power, I suppose I'd still be in that little shop. When we first got into fabricating fuel rods for nuclear reactors, I never dreamed there'd be so much red tape. It's been fifteen years since I've welded. All I do now is push papers."

After breakfast, Ryan left for work. Kim's father said he would work at his office at home.

"Besides," he said half seriously, "they seem to get more done when I'm not around."

Ryan went to the main office and filled out the forms for his employment. He was issued a film badge that would monitor the dose of radioactivity he would be exposed to.

A supervisor gave him a tour of the plant. It seemed like something from science fiction. Operators stood behind lead-lined partitions and manipulated remote-controlled mechanical arms and fingers, loading small pellets of plutonium into the eight-foot-long rods and then welding the ends shut. The rods were then ready to be shipped.

After the tour, they went to a cafeteria for a break. "What do you want me to do?" Ryan asked, sipping his root beer.

"We'll put you on checking the X rays of the welds," the supervisor said, taking a long sip from his cup. "You know, this company has been good to us. This was a poor area before, but now there's jobs. Our kids get good medical care. We can send 'em away to college if they want. Most of us own shares in it. We sort of think of it as our company."

They walked back to the plant, to where the X rays of the welds were inspected. The supervisor showed Ryan an X ray and pointed out a white patch which indicated a welding flaw. "The contract says that all welding flaws will be repaired but, to tell you the truth, when we signed the contract, we didn't really know what we were getting into. We've found out that even when a flaw shows up on the X ray, it doesn't make the weld any less watertight. So when it's a small flaw, we just let 'em go through."

"Oh," Ryan said.

"Fact is we can't make a profit unless we reject fewer than 5 percent of the welds."

"But what about the X rays?" Ryan asked. "There's still the record of the flaw on the X ray."

"You're pretty smart, aren't you," the supervisor said, walking to a desk. "I'm going to show you one of the most important tools in this place. It's made us a profit." He opened a drawer and pulled out a black felt-tip pen.

Ryan looked at the pen for several seconds and then it dawned on him what the supervisor was showing him. "You mark the X ray so the flaw isn't visible?"

"You catch on fast. That's what we do. C'mon here. I'll show you how it's done." With one small mark, the flaw on the X ray disappeared. "Now all you have to do is sign it." Ryan signed his name.

Before he left, the supervisor introduced him to Jesse Colson, a hard-boned, tough-talking man who also checked X rays. Then the supervisor left.

"Just do what I do, and you won't have no trouble," Jesse glumly suggested.

One day during his second week of work, he had just put one of the X rays on the reject pile when Jesse stopped him. "What are you doing?"

"Rejecting it. Look at it for yourself."

"I don't need to look at it. Let it go through."

Ryan looked up at Jesse's hard face. "We can reject 5 percent."

"Why bother to put the welders to all that extra work, when we can fix it right here." Jesse took out his pen and made a small mark, covering up the flaw. He dropped it in the pass box. "If you're planning to reject more than two a week, you talk to me about it first," he demanded.

On Sunday, Ryan attended the Gospel Doctrine class with Kim. Several questions were asked and since nobody else seemed to volunteer, Ryan answered. Finally, near the end of the class, the teacher broke into a broad grin and quipped, "I see we have somebody here who has all the answers. What am I doing here teaching the class? This Yankee friend of Kim's ought to be."

On the way home Kim leaned her head against his shoulder and sighed happily.

"What's that for?" he asked.

"You. You're handsome and smart and good. Do you

know what one of the elderly ladies told me today after Sunday School? She said that you looked to her like the next bishop."

"She shouldn't have said that," Ryan said firmly. Still, he was flattered. She could be right, he thought to himself.

Monday after work, he stopped by the library and checked out a book dealing with nuclear reactors. After retiring to his room for the night, he stayed up past midnight studying the design of a nuclear power reactor. He wanted to know what happened to the fuel rods after they left the plant, and, even if he wouldn't admit it, he wanted to know what would happen in a reactor if a fuel rod leaked through one of the welding flaws that he had passed.

On Wednesday he was asked to give a talk in sacrament meeting. He spent several hours during the week in preparation. Once he caught himself thinking, how would a future bishop give this talk?

After he had given the talk on Sunday, several people came up and complimented him. One of them was the elders quorum president, who also asked him if he would accept an assignment to be a home teacher. Ryan accepted the assignment.

What had started as a little annoyance grew as the days passed. Every time he signed his name to pass a weld that should have been rejected, his guilt grew.

He talked to Kim's father one night about it. "Did you know that some of the welds that have flaws are being passed?"

"Are they?" Kim's father said with little interest.

"Don't you think that's important?"

"Not really. The work we turn out is the best in the industry."

"But I have to sign my name even when I know there's a flaw."

"Don't worry," his future father-in-law advised, "it's only red tape. In business, you have to take shortcuts."

Ryan had assigned to him a fifteen-year-old as a companion for home teaching, but by the time Ryan thought about it, his companion was on vacation, and it was the last of the month. That Saturday afternoon, he took Kim with him. They visited three of the four families assigned to him and idly chatted about weather and gardens.

"You'll have to show me where this other family lives," Ryan said, showing Kim the name and address of the last family.

"Oh, why did they have to give you him?" she asked. "He never comes out to church."

"Do you know where he lives?" Ryan asked, looking at the name, Zeke Stone.

"Oh, Ryan, do we have to go there? It's up some country road. Who knows how to get there, and he won't even care if we go or not." She leaned close to him. "C'mon, let's go swimming."

"Okay," he said.

Two days later, he got a phone call from the elders quorum president about his home teaching. "How'd you do?"

"Got 'em all," Ryan said, resolving that next month he really would visit Zeke Stone, the man who lived in the hills.

That week they sent out their wedding announcement. It showed a picture of the Washington Temple.

The next Sunday, after sacrament meeting, the elders quorum president asked if he could talk with Ryan for a while. Kim agreed to wait for him, whispering into his ear, "I just know it's about the vacancy in the elders quorum presidency."

The quorum president and Ryan found an empty room and sat down opposite each other on folding chairs. The president was a big man, a farmer, one who had a hard time conducting quorum business, always a little self-conscious about his lack of schooling. He began with a prayer.

"You know, I was out shopping for groceries yesterday and I saw Brother Stone." Speaking softly, almost apologetically, he continued, "Well, I asked him how he liked his new home teachers and he said he'd never seen you." The president cleared his throat and fumbled with his clipboard. "Now, I'm not very good at records, but I've written down here that you visited him. I must have made a mistake, don't you think?"

Suddenly he looked into Ryan's eyes, and Ryan knew that he knew that there had been no mistake. Ryan felt the sweat pouring down his arms. He covered his mouth with one hand and looked down at the floor. He felt tears streaking down his face, and it seemed that there was a fist inside his throat. He swallowed hard and whispered, "Could I get a drink of water?"

"Sure, son," the president answered gently.

Ryan rushed to the fountain and let the cool water rush over his face and mouth. Pulling out a handkerchief, he wet it and wiped his brow.

He turned around. The quorum president stood to his left a few feet away, and Kim stood on his right. They both seemed to want to come closer to help him, but neither knew what to say.

"I've lied to the Lord," he agonized. "We never visited Zeke Stone. We went swimming instead."

The president cleared his throat and said quietly, "We all make mistakes. It takes a big man to admit he's done wrong."

Ryan turned to Kim. "Appearances . . . I'm tired of putting up appearances. Covering flaws, pretending they're not real. Pretending to be something I'm not. I need to worry about my own repenting."

Suddenly Kim ran into his arms and held him close to her.

The quorum president touched his shoulder. "It was partly my fault. I should've shown you how to get there. It's not easy to find."

"Can we go up there now?" Ryan asked.

"Sure we can. Let's go now."

They drove Kim home and then headed out of town. They followed the highway for a few miles, then turned onto a county road, and then followed a rutted dirt road. At one point the road veered sharply upward, crossed railroad tracks, and then sunk rapidly downward.

"I'd hate to hit that going fast," Ryan observed.

Then they turned off the dirt road onto a path. The thick growth of bushes and trees closed in around them as they continued, and the branches slapped at the sides of the car as they passed. Suddenly they were out of the green tunnel and into a clearing near the top of the hill.

Zeke Stone was working his garden. He was an old man, wearing faded bib overalls and a tattered hat to shade his face. A battered pickup truck stood beside a small, weatherbeaten house. There was no screen door on the house, and chickens roamed in and out the door. A large dog came running and barking toward them. The quorum president honked his horn and got out to greet Brother Stone. The dog's paws landed on his chest as he gave his greetings.

"Look at that!" Brother Stone shouted with delight. "I got visitors from the Church." He called his dog away from them.

They all stood by the garden and talked. Ryan listened with admiration to their talk, loose, full of laughter and good feelings.

Brother Stone loaded them down with freshly picked corn and tomatoes. Then he invited them over to the shady part of his house, where he had set up two car seats outside.

Going inside, he brought out a banjo, a jar of homemade grape juice, and three cups. While they sat and drank, he tuned up his banjo and played.

The quorum president tapped his feet, chuckling at the endless variations of "Cripple Creek," while Ryan merely sat and smiled.

"You unhappy?" Brother Stone asked Ryan.

"No, sir."

"Then loosen up. You look like a Yankee."

Monday morning at work, Ryan rejected welds that were outside the tolerances set in the contract. By ten o'clock, there were ten rejected X rays on his desk.

"What do you think you're doing?" Jesse snarled when he discovered the rejected welds. "You can't reject all these."

"Look at the X rays."

Suddenly Ryan was being pulled to his feet by his shoulders, and then found himself staring into Jesse's clenched fist.

"Jesse, let go of me," Ryan said quietly.

He dropped his hold. "Change the X rays."

"No, I won't."

"Then get out of here! I'm warning you! All I got to do is make one phone call to my friends and you won't make it out of here in one piece."

"I won't be part of a lie," Ryan said firmly.

"Then quit, walk out while you still can."

Ryan stood, squared away to fight if he had to, his mind racing at what choice to make. Finally he said, "Okay, Jesse. I don't belong here anyway."

As he turned to walk away, Jesse called after him, "If you ever tell anyone about the way we work here, you'll regret it."

That evening Kim and Ryan went to the meetinghouse to be interviewed for temple recommends. The wedding was less than a week away. Ryan was elated to answer one of the bishop's questions, "Are you honest in your dealings with your fellowmen?"

Over the next few days, he tried looking for other work, but there wasn't anything else — or else people in the town, hearing about what they considered his betrayal of the company, wouldn't talk to him about a job.

And at night, Ryan and Kim's father seemed to be constantly dueling, either about the company or else about Kim's affection. Ryan was careful to limit these discussions to times when Kim was not in the room, for he hadn't told her yet about the circumstances which led to his quitting.

"Doesn't it bother you that you're sending defective fuel rods out of your plant?" Ryan asked one evening in the office at home.

"What makes you a sudden expert on nuclear power?" his future father-in-law countered.

"Okay," Ryan admitted, "I'm not an engineer. But why bother to do the X rays at all, then?"

"Because it's in the contract."

"And why is it in the contract?" Ryan pressed.

"Red tape. It's just another form to fill out."

Finally, having looked for work and failed, Ryan asked Kim the inevitable question one morning three days before the wedding. "What would you think about us going back West after we're married?"

"You'll find work, I know you will. You haven't asked Daddy to help you."

"I don't want his help," Ryan answered sharply.

"Why didn't you stay at the job you had?" Kim asked.

"I don't want to talk about it."

"We've got to talk about it. If I'm going to be your wife, I've got to know what's wrong. You and Daddy hardly talk to each other anymore. What's wrong?"

"Okay, Kim, I'll tell you. They're covering up their

mistakes. Some of the fuel rods are being passed with defects in them. It violates their contract."

"That can't be true. Daddy would never let that happen."

"He knows, Kim. I told him. He says it isn't important."

"Then it isn't important," Kim defended.

"It's dishonest."

"Ryan, I won't have you talking like that about my father."

"What do you want for a husband? A cardboard cutout that you can prop up smiling for all social occasions? I can't be like that. You've got to decide between your father or me, but you can't have both of us."

She stormed away from him. He went to his room and started packing slowly, hoping that there was a way to get around the problem, hoping she would come in and apologize, hoping that her father would apologize, trying to remember what the bishop had said about marriage in the interview.

A few minutes later, Kim knocked on his door. He opened it quickly. "There's a phone call for you," she said.

He went to the hall phone to answer it. Kim followed him. "My name is Porter. I'm from the U.S. Nuclear Regulatory Commission. I wonder if I could talk to you for a few minutes . . . unofficially. I'm staying at the motel just outside of town . . . "

He put the phone down. Kim stood across the hall from him.

"What's wrong?" she asked.

"Somebody from the U.S. Nuclear Regulatory Commission. Kim, they must know about the welds. Tell your father."

He ran into his room and got his suitcase and ran out to his car. "Where are you going?" Kim cried.

"Do you think I'll have much chance of staying alive

in this town? Everybody's going to think I told the authorities. I'm leaving town as soon as I can."

He drove around to the back of the motel and walked inside, finally finding the room number given by the man on the phone.

"Thank you for coming," the man said. "It's about your job as an inspector of the X rays. Was there anything strange about the inspection procedures?"

"Are you going to close the plant?" Ryan asked.

"Oh, no, nothing like that. There have been a few complaints, and we just wanted to check around."

"There were some irregularities," Ryan said as he began to explain his experience.

When he was finished, the man thanked him and stood up to show him to the door.

"What will you do now?" Ryan asked.

"There's a plane being sent from Washington with several men like myself. We'll conduct a thorough review of the plant's operation. You've been most helpful. I'll keep our little talk unofficial, but it will be useful in our review."

Ryan ran into the motel office to use a pay phone. He called Kim. "Did you tell your father?"

"Yes, but he's not doing anything. He's just sitting there, like he's in shock." With urgency in her voice, Kim said, "He wants to see you."

"Okay, I'll be there in a minute."

As Ryan drove through the sleepy town, he had the feeling that it was a time bomb, set to blow up in his face.

Kim met him at the door and told him that her father was in his office. Ryan found him idly gazing out the window.

"There's a group of government inspectors coming here. Isn't there anything you want to do . . . to prepare for them?"

He turned to face Ryan. "Do you still love my daughter?"

"Yes, sir."

"Then why don't you marry her?"

"I can't stay in this town."

"Then take her out West. I guess there's worse things than Wyoming, aren't there?" he said with a smile.

"She won't go with me," Ryan said glumly. "She loves you too much to leave."

"Let me look into that," Kim's father said confidently. "Tell me, what do you think I ought to do about my company?"

"I think you ought to cooperate with the inspection, find out what's wrong, and then run it the way it should be run."

He studied Ryan intently, then banged his fist on his desk, smiled, and said, "I'm going to do that."

They were interrupted by a phone call from a secretary at the plant. It was a short call and when it was over, Kim's father said simply, "They've arrived."

"I'm worried about some of the guys at the plant. I bet I'm not very popular with them now."

"Tell me their names and I'll call and explain things to them."

Ryan gave him Jesse's name, and he called the plant and asked to speak with Jesse Colson. After several minutes delay, Kim's father asked, "What do you mean he left? Where did he go? Well, did anybody leave with him? Listen, I want the name of every man that left. You get hold of those men and tell them I want to speak with them!"

He hung up, turned to Ryan and said, "They left work."

"I'm leaving town right now."

"No, let me speak to them."

"Tell Kim I'll call her when I get to Wyoming," Ryan said as he ran out of the office to his car.

He turned onto the highway. A few miles out of town, as he rounded a curve, he saw a car parked ahead of him at the side of the road. Suspecting trouble, he turned into a country road. He saw the car start up, pull a U-turn, and head after him. They both raced down the road, dust billowing up after them, so that it became difficult for Ryan to see how far the car was from him, but, on a curve, he turned back and saw that the car was gaining on him.

Then he realized that he'd been on the road before and that if he made the proper sequence of turns from county road to county road, it would lead to Brother Zeke Stone.

A few minutes later, with a plan in mind, Ryan raced up the steep slope of the railroad crossing and bumped across the tracks. Once over the tracks, he slammed on his brakes. As the car came to a stop, he jumped out, ran for the thick foliage, and waited for the other car.

As he had expected, the car had raced up the steep slope. It wasn't until the driver was starting down the other side that he saw Ryan's car parked in the middle of the road. Ryan could see that the driver was Jesse. He slammed on his brakes and veered to the left, just managing to miss Ryan's car.

Jesse bounded out of his car, swearing about nearly getting killed. He ran to the car to see if Ryan was inside and then yelled to two others, "Burn it!" Then Jesse went to his car and pulled out a rifle, looked around, and picked up a CB mike.

Ryan turned around and fought his way through the foliage, heading parallel to the road so that he would cross the lane that led to Brother Stone's place. After about half an hour, he made it there. Brother Stone was outside in his garden. Ryan ran up to him out of breath and scratched from his trek through the woods.

"What's wrong?" Brother Stone asked.

Ryan explained, and then asked, "Can you take me to another town so I can catch a bus back home?"

"Sure I can," Brother Stone said slowly. First he went to his well and filled his radiator with water, saying, "Water leaks a mite," filled his left rear tire with air, "Tires leak a bit too," and started the pickup running. Then he walked slowly to his house. Ryan followed after him, trying to get him to move faster, expecting any minute to see Jesse burst through the clearing with his rifle blazing.

Brother Stone stood in the doorway and scratched his head. "Now let me see. If we drive down there, we're going to pass 'em, and they're going to look inside, and they're going to see you, and then they're going to stop us. How are they going to tell it's you? Because you look like a Yankee. But we're going to fool 'em, aren't we?"

Ryan ended up with a faded pair of coveralls, a pair of crusty old boots, and a checkered long-sleeve shirt.

Brother Stone examined the effect critically. "One more thing," he said with a wry smile. He went to a shelf and pulled down a large brown jug.

They started down the lane. From the lane they turned onto the road, heading opposite the direction of the railroad tracks. Even so, as they turned one corner, there were three cars and a pickup parked off to the side. Four men stood idly by, waiting to walk into the woods. One of the men had a dog.

Brother Stone continued going at the same slow pace. Calmly he directed Ryan, "Now, pick up the jug, and tip it up like you're going to take a drink, and so it covers your face. It's only water, you know. I threw the other stuff away when I got baptized."

When they were past, Brother Stone chuckled softly, "They didn't pay us any attention at all. Son, you're officially a hillbilly."

When they arrived at the town forty miles away and Brother Stone stopped in front of the bus depot, Ryan was at a loss to express his thanks adequately. Finally he thrust out his hand and said, "I'll never forget this."

"Just a sweet ride in the country. There's nothing to thank me for."

Ryan asked him if he'd phone Kim and tell her he was safe. Then he was gone. Several seconds later, Ryan realized he was still holding the jug.

He walked inside and went to the ticket counter. Setting the jug on the counter, he asked the attendant, "When's the next bus north?"

The man looked at him critically and demanded, "You got any money?"

Ryan looked down at his clothes, then to the jug, then to the man, and burst out laughing. Regaining his composure finally, he fished into the front pocket, pulled out his wallet, and showed the man some money.

Ryan bought a ticket, sat down, and waited. He gazed blankly at the floor, going over in his mind the events of the past few weeks, wondering if he'd ever see Kim again.

A man sat down beside him and whispered, "Mind if I have a drink from your jug?"

Ryan nodded absently.

The man took a drink and spat it out. "What *is* that?"

"Water," Ryan answered.

The bus was on time. Ryan found the first empty row and sat down. He wanted to be alone.

A minute later, as the bus headed down the narrow two-lane road, someone was standing next to him. "Excuse me, I believe you're sitting in my place."

He looked up and saw Kim standing there. In shock, he stood up so she could sit beside him.

"What's in the jug?" she asked suspiciously.

"Water. Kim, why are you on this bus?"

"Because Brother Stone phoned and told us where you were, and because this bus goes through our town one hour before it gets here, and because Daddy is happier now than I've seen him for a long time because he's got a job of rebuilding to do, and because he told me that if I let you go I was a fool—'That boy is honest and I'd trust him with anything'—and because my mother is riding in the bus four rows back . . . "

"Your mother is riding on a bus?" Ryan asked incredulously.

Kim nodded her head. "And because I love you, and I'll stick with you even if you want to raise rutabagas in Iceland. Basically I'd say that's why I'm on this bus."

He carefully set his jug on the floor, leaned over, and kissed her.

A few seats back he could vaguely hear the sound of a woman clearing her throat nervously several times.